"I just think you should be careful, Kathryn. Be very careful."

A cold shiver shimmied along her nerve endings. "That sounds like a warning."

"It is. New Orleans is a fascinating city, but it's dangerous, as well. And you never know where the danger may come from."

"If there's something I should know, Roark, please tell me."

He shook his head. "That's it. I just worry about a beautiful woman alone in a big city."

But that wasn't it. He'd wanted to say more, but something had stopped him. Was it the city she should fear? Or was it Roark with his sensual touch and dark, mysterious eyes?

She would have to be very, very careful. There was no room for mistakes. And no room for any kind of attraction to Roark Lansing.

Dear Harlequin Intrigue Reader,

Summer lovin' holds not only passion, but also danger! Splash into a whirlpool of suspense with these four new titles!

Return to the desert sands of Egypt with your favorite black cat in *Familiar Oasis*, the companion title in Caroline Burnes's FEAR FAMILIAR: DESERT MYSTERIES miniseries. This time Familiar must help high-powered executive Amelia Corbet, who stumbles on an evil plot when trying to save her sister. But who will save Amelia from the dark and brooding desert dweller who is intent on capturing her for his own?

Ann Voss Peterson brings you the second installment in our powerhouse CHICAGO CONFIDENTIAL continuity. Law Davies is not only an attorney, but an undercover agent determined to rescue his one and only love from a dangerous cult—and he is *Laying Down the Law*.

Travel with bestselling author Joanna Wayne to the American South as she continues her ongoing series HIDDEN PASSIONS. In *Mystic Isle*, Kathryn Morland must trust a sexy and seemingly dangerous stranger—who is actually an undercover ex-cop!—to help her escape from the Louisiana bayou alive!

And we are so pleased to present you with a story from newcomer Kasi Blake that is as big as Texas itself! Two years widowed, Julia Keller is confronted on her Texas ranch by a lone lawman with the face of her dead beloved husband. Is he really her long-lost mate and father of her child—or an impostor? That is the question for this *Would-Be Wife*.

Enjoy all four!

Denise O'Sullivan
Associate Senior Editor
Harlequin Intrigue

MYSTIC ISLE
JOANNA WAYNE

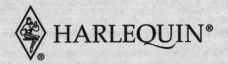

TORONTO • NEW YORK • LONDON
AMSTERDAM • PARIS • SYDNEY • HAMBURG
STOCKHOLM • ATHENS • TOKYO • MILAN • MADRID
PRAGUE • WARSAW • BUDAPEST • AUCKLAND

ISBN 0-373-22675-6

MYSTIC ISLE

Copyright © 2002 by JoAnn Vest

Printed in U.S.A.

ABOUT THE AUTHOR

Joanna Wayne lives with her husband just a few miles from steamy, exciting New Orleans, but her home is the perfect writer's hideaway. A lazy bayou, complete with graceful herons, colorful wood ducks and an occasional alligator, winds just below her back garden. When not creating tales of spine-tingling suspense and heartwarming romance, she enjoys reading, traveling, playing golf and spending time with family and friends.

Joanna believes that one of the special joys of writing is knowing that her stories have brought enjoyment to or somehow touched the lives of her readers. You can write Joanna at P.O. Box 2851, Harvey, LA 70059-2851.

Books by Joanna Wayne

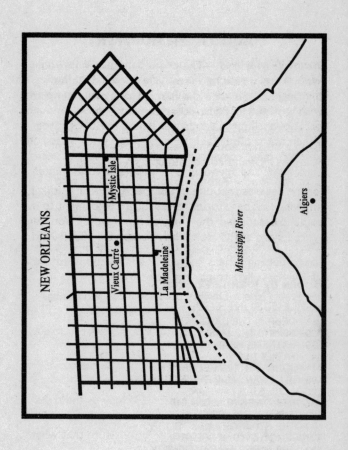

NEW ORLEANS

Mystic Isle

Vieux Carré •

La Madeleine

Mississippi River

Algiers •

CAST OF CHARACTERS

Kathryn Morland—The practical, responsible young woman has pulled her sister out of one jam after another, but this time she may have followed her into a web of danger that neither can escape.

Roark Lansing—Mysterious and incredibly sexy, he is on a mission and only death can stop him—until Kathryn Morland comes along.

Lisa Morland—Kathryn's impetuous sister, who has jumped into a bizarre world of illusions where nothing is what it seems and death and danger are the only realities.

Devlin Tishe—A charismatic leader who devotes his life to helping others find peace and harmony as long as they're willing to pay the price.

Veretha Tishe—Devlin's provocative wife, who has a taste for the exotic and dangerous.

Cottonmouth—The guard of the manor who makes sure everyone is watched very carefully.

Detective Butch Ranklin—A homicide detective with a personal interest in finding a killer.

Raycine Ranklin—She came too close to the truth and it cost her her life.

Punch—A homeless teenager who is sure that what she knows can get her killed.

Prologue

New Orleans, Louisiana
October 31

The music throbbed, surging through her body, flooding her senses. She let its hypnotic rhythm possess her, embrace her as the love swelled in her. No one had ever understood her pain, the loneliness and grief she so desperately longed to escape. No one, not even her sister. No one, until Devlin Tishe.

He smiled and new energy erupted inside her. She felt alive, fluid and sensual, like the strange music that drove her. Like the drums that beat in time to the rushing of her blood. The silky fabric of the loose veils fell about her body, brushing her skin, hugging her breasts like a lover, dipping and caressing the heated flesh of her thighs.

Effortlessly she twirled about the room, her bare feet skimming the tiled floor. Devlin's dark eyes followed her every move, his mere gaze more fulfilling than any ordinary man's lovemaking had ever been. The two of them, alone with only the heat of unspoken desires and the knowledge that after tonight nothing would be the same again. She would truly enter his world, and Lisa

Morland would become only a memory. Lizemera would be born.

She swayed closer to Devlin, dancing so near that the soft fabric of her veils touched his skin, too, brushing across his arm and the dark hairs on his muscled chest. Slowly he reached out to her, his hand skimming across her skin, and desire burned inside her.

She lowered her body, twisting and turning like the beautiful snake Devlin had shown her. And now his hands had become part of her dance, part of the magic that was setting her free. He pulled her body closer and touched his lips to the soft flesh of her belly.

The room began to spin, a carousel of flickering lights and exotic scents, a circle of harmony. She was one with herself. And one with Devlin.

Suddenly a new figure entered the room. Lisa shivered, the desire and freedom that had welled up inside her fighting the cruel intrusion of reality. Devlin had promised they would be alone tonight. It was her transformation, her special time with the master.

But now Veretha stood in the doorway, her coal-black hair falling over her creamy shoulders, her eyes as dark and as dangerous as the unprotected night.

"Come with me, Lizemera." Her voice was low, but insistent. "Your time with Devlin is over. The spirits await you."

Lisa looked to Devlin, but his eyes no longer held assurance.

"I'm afraid she's right, my beautiful Lizemera. Everything has its season."

Veretha motioned once more to Lisa, then turned and led the way into the mysterious unknown.

Chapter One

New Orleans, Louisiana
December 1

Kathryn Morland drummed her well-manicured nails on the leather briefcase that rested in her lap. Pushing back the sleeve of her blazer, she glanced at her watch. Four-forty-five. Five more minutes would make two solid hours that the New Orleans police force had vacillated between giving her the runaround and ignoring her completely.

Her patience was wearing paper-thin.

So far this afternoon she'd endured a bumpy flight from Dallas to New Orleans and suffered through the incompetence of an unconcerned sergeant. She'd practically had to threaten the man with a lawsuit to even get him to listen to her missing-person's complaint. Now, to top it off, she'd been crammed into this foul-smelling cubicle and forgotten.

Her finger drumming grew louder. The promised detective was probably out there drinking another cup of coffee and hoping she'd just give up and leave. If she had half a brain she would. Lisa had pulled these pouting and disappearing acts before. Only this time...

A sudden nervousness twisted Kathryn's stomach into a hard knot. This time was different.

"Kathryn Morland?"

She looked up and into the penetrating eyes of the middle-aged black man who'd spoken her name. "I'm Kathryn Morland."

"Detective Ranklin." He poked a large hand in her direction. His hand wrapped around hers firmly, but he didn't take his eyes from her face. Sizing her up, no doubt, to see if she was the delusional nut the desk sergeant had taken her for.

"Sergeant Blakely says you're in town trying to find your sister."

"That's right. I gave the details of her disappearance to him."

"I've got it all right here." Ranklin held the forms in his right hand and waved them about, circulating the rancid air. "Now why don't you step into my office and we'll talk about it?" he offered, turning to guide her through an open door that led down a narrow hall.

She followed him, eventually stepping into another cubicle, slightly larger than the one she had been in, but still barely big enough to hold a desk, a steel gray file cabinet and a couple of chairs. A picture of an attractive woman and a striking, much younger woman sat on Ranklin's desk amid piles of clutter.

Kathryn plowed right in before there was time for more small talk. "I'm very concerned about my sister's disappearance."

"I understand. It's always frightening when a family member drops out of sight," Ranklin answered. He walked over and removed a stack of folders and an empty McDonald's bag from a metal folding chair and motioned her to have a seat.

She brushed away a few crumbs and sat. Ranklin ignored her while he skimmed the report he held in his hand. Finally he slid the papers to his desk and dropped in a heavy heap to the swivel chair behind his desk.

"So tell me," he said, his deep voice filling every corner of the small room. "Your sister is almost twenty-five years old, definitely old enough to be on her own. What makes you think she's in trouble?"

Because Lisa was always in trouble. Because she hadn't called home at Thanksgiving. Because an anonymous caller in the middle of the night said she was. Those were true, but probably wouldn't nudge the detective into action. Actually Kathryn wasn't sure anything would, but she'd wasted an afternoon on the police already. She might as well give them first crack.

"My sister moved to New Orleans three months ago. Now she seems to have disappeared."

"According to this report, you haven't had any contact in over a month."

So he had paid at least some attention to the report. Her confidence lifted a hairbreadth. "Not since a few days before Halloween." Kathryn knotted her hands. "That's the reason I'm worried."

"Did anything significant happen the last time you talked? You know, an argument, harsh words, some indication she was in trouble?"

"Yes. When she called, she asked me to advance her ten thousand dollars of her trust fund."

"That's a lot of money." Ranklin shuffled some papers around on his desk and located a legal-size notepad. "Did she say why she needed ten grand?"

"She said it was for an investment and that she needed it immediately. I asked for more details. She said I wouldn't understand."

"Have you had to bail her out of trouble before?"

"I've lent her money on occasion."

Ranklin nodded his head as if she'd made a major confession. "On occasion," he repeated.

Okay, so *on occasion* was the understatement of the year. Kathryn fingered the strap on the briefcase. Kathryn, the rescuer.

"Your sister sounds a little irresponsible. That must be frustrating." Ranklin picked up a nub of a pencil and scribbled a few notes on the pad. "And you have no idea why she needed the money?"

"No, but even before that call, I could tell that something was wrong. She'd become distant, barely talking when I called her and never calling me."

"Did she have a boyfriend?"

"I don't know. When she first moved to New Orleans, she seemed fascinated with the homeless youngsters who lived on the streets. Then all of a sudden, the talk switched to almost fanatical ravings about a harmonious life she'd discovered and some wonderful man named Devlin Tishe. He sounded like some kind of nut to me, and I told her as much."

"How did she react to that?"

"She got angry. After a while she quit talking about him at all, but I think she was still involved with him. She gets caught up in these things easily. She never wants my advice until she's in over her head."

"Impetuous and a tad gullible, huh. I've had some experience with that myself." A slight smile curved Ranklin's lips, but didn't reach his eyes. "It can be disturbing, but usually there's no cause for alarm."

"You don't understand—" she protested, but he stopped her short.

"Believe me, I understand. It happens to all of us.

We do and do for someone we love, and they turn on us when we try to help. Have you asked Devlin Tishe about your sister?''

"I called Mystic Isle and talked to a woman named Veretha.''

"Veretha Tishe. That would be his wife.''

"She never mentioned that, and I certainly never got the impression from Lisa that Devlin Tishe was married.''

"He's married. I'm not sure what that means in his case, but he does have a wife. Did she talk to you?''

"Yes. She was friendly until I mentioned Lisa's name. Then her attitude changed abruptly.''

"How so?''

"She said she didn't remember anyone by that name. I insisted she let me talk to Devlin. Apparently he was not in right then and when he finally called me back, he admitted that he knew Lisa. He said she'd attended a few lectures at Mystic Isle, but that he hadn't seen her in weeks.''

"I get the impression you didn't believe him.''

"I have my doubts, especially since I checked into his background a little more. From what I could find out, he operates out of some old house on the edge of the French Quarter and that he pretends to be a spiritual leader of sorts. The giveaway was that he has a voodoo shop on the premises. Mystic Isle. That's where I called when I got Veretha.''

"Actually it's the entire operation that's known as Mystic Isle.''

"And does the city just let him do as he pleases, Detective?''

"As far as I'm concerned, the world would be a

better place without the likes of Devlin Tishe, but he's not breaking any laws. At least none that we know of."

"Unless I'm seriously mistaken, he tried to milk ten thousand dollars from my sister and is involved in her disappearance. What does it take to break the law around here?"

"Killing, stealing and parking in a tow-away zone, not necessarily in that order." Ranklin worked on his smile again. "Other than that, we pretty much try to live and let live. The First Amendment, you know. Tishe might persuade a lot of gullible people into believing his hype and donating their hard-earned money to supporting his lifestyle, but he's not physically dangerous. And from what I read in the report, you have no real reason to suspect foul play. My guess is that your sister is fine."

Kathryn scooted to the front edge of her chair. "My sister is *not* fine. She's missing." Her voice rose several decibels. "The investigator that I'd hired talked to Lisa's landlady. She said Lisa came home on the afternoon of October 31, packed her things and moved out without giving any notice and without leaving a forwarding address."

"So you have hired a private investigator?"

"He's no longer working the case."

"I see. What about her work? Did your sister quit her job?"

"She didn't work. She lived on a small monthly stipend from her trust fund and on money I gave her."

"Where is that money being mailed?"

"To her old address. The checks were returned undelivered."

"So she hasn't cashed a check since October 31 and no one has admitted hearing from her since that date?"

"I'm not certain."

"Why don't you explain that answer for me."

She took a deep breath. Kathryn had deliberately left this out of the missing-persons report, had been hesitant to mention the facts surrounding her sister's trust fund. But she realized now she couldn't expect action unless she gave the NOPD the full truth.

"Our parents died in a plane crash five years ago. They left us an operating software company and the family home. There was little cash and barely enough insurance to bury them. All the money had gone into building the business. But our maternal grandmother left both of us sizable trust funds to be collected on our twenty-fifth birthday. Lisa will be twenty-five on December 8."

Ranklin glanced at his calendar. "Seven days from today."

"Exactly. The attorney who oversees the trust fund got a phone call from someone claiming to be Lisa two weeks ago. The caller requested that the money be sent to a bank in New Orleans in the form of a cashier's check. She wanted the check to arrive on December 8."

"How did the attorney react to that?"

"He refused the request. He informed the caller that the check had to be picked up in his office by Lisa herself. Then he asked her to answer a few questions that Lisa would have had no trouble answering in order to verify her identity. The caller was able to give Lisa's social security number and birth date, but when he asked things of a more personal nature, like questions about her family, she hung up the phone."

"And that led him to believe that the caller wasn't Lisa."

"That and the fact that he didn't think it sounded like her. The attorney is also a family friend who's known both of us all our lives. The caller could have been anyone who knew about the trust fund. She might either have Lisa's identification or have fake ID. It's easy enough to come by these days."

"Far too easy. So did the caller agree to the attorney's terms?"

"Not then. She called back two days later asking that the check be ready for pickup on December 8."

"Then I don't know what you have to worry about. If your sister is meeting with the attorney in his office, she must be fine."

"There's more. A week ago I received a phone call in the middle of the night, eleven minutes after two to be exact. The caller was a young woman, hysterical and out of breath, as if she'd been running or was very frightened."

"Did she identify herself?"

"No, didn't even give me a chance to ask her name. All she said was that Lisa was in danger, that she'd be dead before her birthday unless I got her out of that place. Then she screamed and the connection was broken."

"Why didn't you call us then?"

"I thought it was some kind of hoax."

"So you ignored the call."

"No. That's when I hired a private investigator to find Lisa."

"And then you fired him?"

"I let him go."

"What did he find out while he was on the case?"

"No more than I already knew, that Lisa hadn't been seen or heard from since before Halloween." She sucked in a deep breath of stale air. "And that's why I'm here today. I'm convinced this is all connected to Devlin Tishe. For all I know he and his wife may be keeping her locked away somewhere while they try to find a way to get their hands on her money."

"Exactly how much is this trust fund worth?"

"Just under twelve million dollars."

Ranklin pursed his lips and let out a low whistle. "That's a lot of money, and that does change the picture. There are plenty of lowlifes in this town who'd kidnap the pope himself for that kind of money. Kidnap or worse."

Kathryn shivered, as cold as if the window had been flung open to let in a freezing blast. She knew her sister could be dead, but she couldn't think that way now. If she did, she'd give in to the grief and become incapable of doing what had to be done.

Ranklin eased from his chair and walked over to lean his backside on the front side of his desk, a few inches from Kathryn's chair. "We'll do what we can to help you locate your sister, Miss Morland, but in the meantime, try to take it easy. According to the report you filled out, there's been no ransom note."

"I almost wish there had been. Then at least I might have some idea what I'm up against. It would also help if I knew what Tishe and his wife are capable of."

"Like I said, the man has never been accused of so much as a misdemeanor, much less a kidnapping."

"There's always a first time." Her tone was razor-sharp. She no longer cared. "I think Lisa is in danger, but I can see I won't get any help from the police. Maybe if she'd parked in a tow-away zone."

"I never said we wouldn't look for her." Ranklin's gaze caught and held hers. "I'm sure there are people

besides Devlin Tishe who know about her trust fund.
Did she mention having told anyone in New Orleans
about it? Anyone at all?''

"No, but I'm sure she would have told Devlin. Wife
or no wife, I got the distinct impression that she was
having an affair with him. She was totally taken with
the man and with his bizarre doctrine.''

"The trust fund does add a few twists to the situation, but you seem like an intelligent, practical woman,
Miss Morland. You don't know how I appreciate that,
considering some of the loonies I deal with in this
town. That's why I have hope that you're going to do
the smart thing.''

"Which is?''

"Go back to Dallas and leave this investigation to
the police. Stay away from Tishe and Mystic Isle. It's
no place for a woman like you." Ranklin walked over
and opened the door. "We have your home and cell-
phone number in the report. We'll be in touch.''

Kathryn murmured her insincere thanks for what she
was sure was nothing and pushed through the door.
She'd done the sensible thing, gone to the police first
and tried to recruit their help. Now she was on her own.
If she hurried, she could make it to Mystic Isle before
dark.

BUTCH RANKLIN watched Kathryn Morland make her
exit. About five and half feet, dark-blond hair that was
straight and shiny and didn't quite make it to her shoulders, a shapely body. The view was pleasant—the only
nice thing that had happened today. The bad had started
at breakfast with his wife's updated top-ten list of complaints. The worse part was, most of them were probably legitimate.

Too little money. Too little time for her. Too little sex. Too little everything except work. Most of all she was upset over the ultimatum he'd given his daughter Raycine a few months ago. Stay in college or get a job and move out. She'd gotten angry and stormed out of the house.

Things hadn't cooled down since. Now they hardly ever heard from her, and his wife was certain Raycine had gotten in with the wrong crowd. She hadn't even come home for Thanksgiving dinner—hadn't even called. Worrying her mother to death, and much as he hated to admit it, he was getting worried, too. So he did understand Kathryn Morland's concern for her sister. Twelve million dollars was a lot of money, especially in a city where people had been killed on the street for a pair of high-priced tennis shoes.

"Hey, Ranklin. The boss is looking for you. Some reporter from Channel Four just called him. They're looking for a statement on last night's double murder on Rampart."

Ranklin frowned at the bad-news bearer. "My statement is that there was a double murder on Rampart last night."

"Tell it to the chief."

Yeah, sure. He would, along with the really big news. He'd narrowed the suspects down to under a few thousand. God, what a city. The good, the bad and the kids with guns.

Jerking open his desk drawer, he rummaged until he located the bottle of antacid pills. He unscrewed the top and shook three into his hand, then tossed them into his mouth. Time to feed the ulcer.

Reaching under the Morland file, he pulled out the one the chief was waiting on. Lisa Morland could be

in real trouble, but he doubted seriously Devlin Tishe
was at the root of it. As far as Ranklin was concerned
Tishe was no more than a piece of crab shell floating
in a gumbo of real problems—like murders, armed rob-
beries and child molesters. If people wanted to give
him their money, that was their problem. Hell, it wasn't
much worse than gambling it away at the casinos or
spending it on strippers and booze in the French Quarter.

The phone on Ranklin's desk rang. He ignored it.
The boss was waiting.

THE CABDRIVER FOLLOWED Kathryn's instructions,
pulling to the curb and letting her out a block away
from Mystic Isle. A walk in the brisk air should clear
her mind and let her come up with a workable plan of
action.

Of course, she *could* just march right in and an-
nounce she was Lisa's sister and demand that they tell
her what they knew about her disappearance. The direct
approach. That was the way she liked to do things. But
there was no reason to think they wouldn't lie to her
in person the same way they had on the phone. Lisa
had done a lot more than attend a few of Devlin's lectures. That much Kathryn was sure of.

A chilling breeze hit Kathryn in the face, and she
picked up her pace, walking quickly past a row of magnificent old houses with iron balconies and shuttered
windows. She'd found the location of Mystic Isle in
the phone book. It was on Esplanade, a fascinating avenue on the edge of the French Quarter, a place where
the old and new met but never fully merged. Or maybe
they did, she decided, catching sight of the black-and-
silver sign that welcomed visitors to Mystic Isle.

The three-story mansion with its huge porches and balconies and topped by a turret, was almost Gothic. The paint was faded and peeling. Stately oaks lined the walk, their branches painting the path in a patchwork of forbidding shadows.

Squaring her shoulders, she marched up the steps, through a large, wooden door and into the world of Devlin Tishe.

Chapter Two

Soft chimes announced Kathryn's entry into a high-ceilinged foyer containing bizarre sculptures and wooden statues. Candles flickered on an antique table, their light reflecting from the framed mirror behind them. Slowly her eyes adjusted to the dimness, and she made her way into the next room.

The new surroundings caught her off guard, and for a moment all she could do was stand and stare. Crystal chandeliers, dimmed to a faint glow, hung from the high ceilings, bathing the spacious room in soft light and lengthening shadows. The carpet was a pale blue, as deep and inviting as the Gulf of Mexico, and over-stuffed chairs and tables of dark wood filled every corner of the room. The place was definitely unlike any voodoo shop she'd ever imagined. Cleaner. Far more luxurious.

There was a display of tarot cards on mahogany shelves along the wall, with decks set out on small round tables surrounded by comfortable chairs. Unique voodoo-type dolls of all sizes stared from behind a domed glass case, and numerous books on spells and potions were neatly displayed on dust-free shelves.

Bottles and bags of potions filled huge wicker baskets that were scattered about the room.

"Welcome to Mystic Isle."

Kathryn jumped and spun around to find the owner of the deep male voice standing a few feet away, staring openly at her.

"I didn't mean to startle you," he said, stepping closer.

"I'm fine. I guess I was just absorbed in the atmosphere."

"Yes, this is a special place. Are you looking for something in particular, or perhaps you only want to take a reprieve from the troubled world?"

Kathryn stared, too surprised for a sensible response. The man was good, she'd give him that. The smooth baritone of his voice alone would convince most customers he had something they needed. And if the customer happened to be female, the man's dark good looks would definitely loosen the purse strings—for whatever he was selling.

"I'm just looking," she lied. "Are you the owner of this shop?"

"No. Devlin Tishe and his wife, Veretha, are the owners. I'm merely here to greet you and make you feel welcome while you explore our world."

He smiled, half mysterious, half inviting. She let her gaze slide the length of his body, down the coarse denim of his black shirt that opened halfway to his waist, revealing smooth, bronzed skin and a lush field of dark hair. Past the low waistline of his black jeans to the rough leather of the boots that climbed nearly to his knees.

Shifting her feet and the direction of her gaze, she studied the flawless features of his face. It was important that she find out everything she could about Tishe and the people who worked for him. Besides, she was sure this man wouldn't mind her stares. He was no doubt part of the ambience, designed to help separate the customers from their senses and their cash.

"You look a little puzzled," he said. "Maybe you were expecting something else?"

"I'm not sure what I was expecting." This time she spoke the truth. But some things were beginning to make a bit more sense. The man, the mesmerizing way he spoke, even the glitzy appearance of the shop. This was one smooth operation, and this was one very sexy man. If Devlin was even sexier, she could easily imagine Lisa becoming infatuated with him.

"Feel free to look around," he said. "And if I can help you, don't hesitate to ask." He extended his right hand. "My name is Roark."

She let his warm hand wrap around hers, squeezing, but not shaking, more an embrace than a handshake. A flush of unexpected warmth crept to her flesh. Even she was getting caught up in the atmosphere. "Is Roark a first or last name?"

"It's Roark Lansing. And now you have the advantage."

"My name is Kathryn…Richards." Damn. She'd almost given her real name. Thank heavens she'd caught herself in time, remembered to give the name she'd used when she'd checked in at the hotel. There were hundreds of Kathryns around. It would take the Morland to connect her with Lisa.

Flashing Roark what she hoped looked like an innocent smile, she turned and walked to one of the round tables in the middle of the room. She had to appear to be the typical first-time visitor. Curious and open, but not too eager. Picking up one of the dolls, she pretended to examine it. "Is there a story behind this doll?"

"It's said that a person skilled in curses can do harm to a living person by putting pins in the doll."

"A voodoo doll. I've heard of them." She placed the doll back on the table. "This is pretty swanky for a voodoo shop."

"We prefer to think of it as a shop where one can find secrets of things not seen, aids for exploring ancient practices and rituals. Were you looking for something in particular?"

"Not really."

"Then make yourself at home. A lot of tourists just come in for a souvenir to take home to their friends. Everyone is welcome and questions are encouraged."

"The ad in the Yellow Pages said Mystic Isle offered classes and instruction in how to achieve harmony in all aspects of your life."

"This is true."

"So if I took one of the classes, could I go out and practice voodoo?"

"Not from what you learn at Mystic Isle. Devlin does not teach or practice voodoo, though he has nothing against it. He focuses on harmony and peace. It's a simple message for those who are seeking true happiness."

"How enlightening." *And what a crock.* Turning her back on Roark, she moved about the room, stopping at each display to examine the merchandise. Roark didn't follow, but she could feel his eyes watching her every move. Feigning interest, she picked up a snake, intricately carved from a piece of solid mahogany. The details were so realistic it seemed to come alive in her hand, and she was struck with the sensation that it was moving, preparing to strike.

"That piece was created by a local craftsman," he explained, walking over to point out the artist's initials on the snake's belly.

His fingers covered hers. In an instant heat suffused her body, flowing from his touch like fingers of fire. The snake fell from her hands.

"It's only a carving. It can't hurt you."

She slipped her shaking hand into her pocket and took a deep breath. God, this place was getting to her. "So tell me more about the teachings of this Devlin Tishe," she said, determined to keep her mind as clear as her mission. "Does he hold regular classes?"

"He does, but they're not for everyone. Frankly, I don't think you'd be interested, Miss Richards. Or is it Mrs.?"

"Ms. will do." So, she wasn't the kind they wanted. Not quite naive enough. It hadn't taken him long to figure that out. Probably because she'd pulled away at his touch. She was sure that didn't happen too often.

The chime over the door sounded again and a group of teenage girls nervously giggled and wiggled their way inside.

"Why don't you just look around now while I see if I can help these young ladies?" Roark said.

Kathryn perused a rack of books on spells and curses, while Roark turned his charms on the newest customers. Then, stopping to examine first one object and then another, Kathryn maneuvered her way to a closed door at the rear of the shop. She turned the knob, opened the door and stepped inside.

The room was more like an oversize closet. Folding metal tables held piles of flyers and pamphlets, and haphazardly stacked cardboard boxes filled every corner. Roark's deep, husky voice and the high-pitched tones of the giddy girls carried from the other room. Kathryn picked up a pamphlet entitled "Finding Peace." She skimmed through it and several others.

Basically, they all said the same thing, that Devlin Tishe had all the answers. She picked up a flyer. Hear Devlin Tishe and change your life. December 1. Tonight. Maybe her luck was changing. She folded the flyer and tucked it inside the pocket of her blazer.

"This area is private."

Kathryn sucked in her breath and swung around. Roark was standing behind her, towering over her and challenging her presence. She held her head high, meeting his stare. There was something there she hadn't seen before. A coldness, or maybe a warning. It didn't matter. She didn't have the option of heeding it.

"I'm sorry. I thought you might keep the special stuff back here. You know, the real charms and potions."

"Whatever you're looking for, you won't find it here."

"I guess not." She eased out the door and back into the main room of the shop, amazed that his attitude had changed so dramatically and so quickly. She started toward the exit.

Roark followed, then stepped in front to open the door and usher her out. "I'm sorry we didn't have anything to interest you," he said, slipping back into his smooth, seductive voice.

"Ah, but you did. I'll see you tonight. At Devlin's meeting."

"That's not a good idea."

"Why is that?"

"Because…" He paused as another customer hurried up the front steps in their direction. "Because it will transform your life." His voice fell to a whisper. "And you may not like the changes."

"I guess that's a chance I'll have to take." Without waiting for a comeback, she turned and hurried down the steps and into the real world.

She didn't believe in spells or curses or sticking pins in voodoo dolls. She didn't even believe in hunches or female intuition ordinarily. Nonetheless, she felt certain that Devlin Tishe or someone at Mystic Isle was involved in Lisa's disappearance. It wouldn't surprise her at all if the villain turned out to be Roark Lansing.

ROARK STOOD in the doorway watching Kathryn Morland march her shapely body down the steps, her soft blond hair bouncing about her shoulders. He hadn't recognized her at first, not until she'd gone snooping on her own. The picture he'd seen of her didn't do her justice.

He wasn't surprised she'd shown up at Mystic Isle. He'd expected her. He'd just hoped it wouldn't be this soon.

Forget that. She was here.

Damn. Where was luck when he needed it? Probably perched on Devlin's shoulder like some smitten, fallen angel, as usual. Roark shoved his fists into his pockets. Forcing the requisite smile to his face, he stepped back inside Mystic Isle—and back inside a situation that was growing more dangerous with every passing day.

KATHRYN SHED her shoes as soon as the bellboy deposited her luggage and left the hotel room. Her feet ached and an irritating throb had taken up residence behind her eyes. The day had been exhausting and had done nothing to alleviate her fears for Lisa. And, now that she thought about it, she'd never stopped for lunch, which might help explain the headache.

She stacked all three of the pillows against the headboard and leaned against them before reaching for the hotel guide that sat on the bedside table. The room-service menu was extensive, offering a wide selection of New Orleans favorites—red beans and rice, crawfish étoufée, seafood gumbo. All dishes that promised to deliver a full burst of hot, spicy flavor.

She'd try all of them if she stayed in town long enough, just as she had on her last trip to the city, but this afternoon, she preferred something bland. Picking up the phone, she ordered a turkey and Swiss sandwich on wheat bread. For the past few days, every bite of food had seemed to stick in her throat, then swell into a hard, lumpy mass when it finally reached her stomach. Anxiety was tough on the digestive system.

Rubbing the back of her neck, she tried for at least the hundredth time to remember exactly what Lisa had said about Devlin. If she'd known it would come down to this, she'd have paid a lot more attention. As it was, all she remembered were bits and pieces of their conversations.

Lisa had been impressed with the man from their first meeting, had gone on and on about how enlightening his ideas were and how he had the answers she'd been searching for. The fact that Lisa had questions had been news to Kathryn. Still, she had taken it as just another of Lisa's infatuations and been totally unimpressed by her ravings.

During the next couple of weeks, Lisa's feelings toward Devlin had changed. She'd talked of him more as a lover than as a teacher, said he was attentive and understanding, that he made her feel things she'd never felt before, that he was more seductive than any man she'd ever known. But Devlin had not been the first man to impress Lisa that way. Kathryn had just assumed the infatuation would wear thin soon, the way it had done every time before.

Impressionable. That was the word their father had frequently used to describe his younger daughter, along with sensitive, vulnerable, delicate. Sometimes Kathryn wondered if her parents' expectations hadn't set Lisa's personality, rather than explain it. A self-fulfilling prophecy that Lisa had embraced eagerly, an excuse not to grow up.

Or maybe it had been Lisa's looks that had shaped her personality. She had been the adorable baby of the family—blond, blue-eyed, cute, little upturned nose. Kathryn had been the awkward, scrawny, three year older sister. She'd been loved, but not spoiled rotten. Now she realized that it had been a blessing in disguise. She had learned to assume responsibility and to take care of herself.

No one could understand why a woman with an inheritance of millions went to work every day, but Kathryn had never considered any other lifestyle. The business needed her and she needed it and the purpose it gave her. She was carrying on her father's dream, developing new educational software that kept children entertained while learning about their world.

Stretching across the bed, she closed her eyes. Old images formed and played like a video in her mind. She was nine years old again, pushing out the back door and into their fenced backyard...

She skipped toward Chaser, sure the black retriever

would jump up and come running to her. Only, he didn't. "Chaser!" *He didn't move.*

She knelt beside him. Flies hovered around his nose and his eyes were open and bulging. She looked up as the back door slammed shut. Lisa skipped toward her, her curls bouncing about her head.

"What's the matter with Chaser?"

"Go away, Lisa. Just go away."

"You can't tell me what to do." Lisa kneeled and put her face next to Chaser's. "He looks weird. Is he sick?"

"Go back inside, Lisa. Please."

"He's dead, isn't he?"

Dead. The word turned her inside out. She tried to push Lisa away, but her sister started to cry. Their father flew out the door, rushing to her rescue, as always. He grabbed Lisa up in his arms. "What's the matter, precious?"

Kathryn forced her thoughts back to the present, angry with herself for letting the bitter memories escape the recesses of her mind. It had been so long ago, and it wasn't Lisa's fault. It wasn't anyone's fault. It was just the way it had been. The way it still was, but no one had forced her to take on the role of Lisa's caretaker after her parents' untimely deaths.

A knock sounded at the door. "Room service."

"One moment." She exhaled sharply, sat up and swung her feet to the floor. The meeting with Lisa's former landlady and then with Roark Lansing had only intensified her conviction that Lisa was in some kind of danger. That was why so much depended on tonight's meeting with Devlin Tishe, the revered teacher of brainwashing bunk.

She'd love to believe he was the wonderful man Lisa

had described, but if he was, why had he lied about their relationship? And why had he seduced Lisa when he had a wife?

One thing was certain. She wouldn't be as gullible as Lisa had been. She'd walk into the meeting tonight with her eyes wide open and her mind sharp. She swung open the door and ushered the food server inside, suddenly ravenous.

KATHRYN TOOK a deep breath and smoothed the lines of her brown flannel skirt as she stepped into the large meeting room on the second floor of Mystic Isle. Scanning the area, she studied the layout. About a hundred metal chairs were set in rows of ten, and at least half of them were already filled.

The crowd was a lot more diverse than she'd anticipated. Young people who looked as if they might sleep on the streets sat next to fashionably clad silver-haired matrons. There was also a sizable contingent of what appeared to be young professionals, as well as a few men in worn jeans or work uniforms. Apparently Devlin Tishe had a remarkably wide appeal.

Unfortunately the crowd did not include Lisa. And there was no sign of Roark Lansing, either.

A dark, exotic-looking woman entered from a side door. An assortment of unusual necklaces and bracelets jangled softly and her hips swayed seductively beneath an ankle-length coral skirt as she made her way toward a small stage in the front of the room. A group of young men gathered around her and she looked like some south-sea island princess holding court with her ardent subjects.

The room continued to fill, and Kathryn considered her seating choices. There were a few spots left in the front half of the room, but they were all in the center of a row, and she'd have to climb over people to get to one of them. She decided on a seat near the back and on the aisle. Before she'd taken more than a few steps in that direction, the room's climate made a drastic change.

The voices dropped to low murmurs and all eyes turned to the front of the room. She could all but feel the anticipation as it swept through the crowd. "It's him," a woman at her elbow whispered. "Devlin Tishe."

Kathryn shifted her gaze for her first glimpse of the famed leader. She wasn't sure what she'd expected, but the imposing figure didn't disappoint. The man was over six feet tall and impeccably dressed in a gray suit that probably cost more than a month's salary of a lot of people in the room. He looked to be in his midfifties, and his salt-and-pepper hair was stylishly short.

He stepped to the platform and the microphone. "If you're here to find peace, you've come to the right place. Please take a seat. The spirits are waiting."

His voice was deep, smooth, hypnotic, and the people who were still standing moved quickly and almost silently to vacant seats. Whatever else he might possess, Tishe had charisma. He emanated power and persuasion the way a radio tower emits high-frequency beams—silent, but intense.

"The spirits are with us tonight," he began. "Evil spirits. Pure spirits. They move among us. Close your eyes and feel their power, experience their struggle inside you as they fight to gain control of your life."

Kathryn listened and observed as Tishe swung into his spiel. There had been a noticeable drop in the temperature and a slow but steady dimming of the lights since he'd come into the room. Apparently Tishe was well versed in the use of physical effects to enhance emotional responses.

She listened intently for the first half hour, then grew restless. His doctrine was fascinating, if far-fetched, a hodgepodge of religions, myths, and a smattering of what sounded like devil worship. And through it all ran the repeated message that Devlin himself held all the secrets for balancing this very eclectic and potentially volatile mixture.

Kathryn studied the faces of the audience. Some looked doubtful, but still appeared to be listening intently. Many more appeared to be mesmerized either by what Tishe said or by the man himself. It was likely that no one would notice if she quietly left the room and used the time to do a little investigating of the physical plant.

Faking a persistent cough, she stood and made her way to the exit, hoping that if any of Tishe's staff noticed her leaving, they'd assume she was going in search of a water fountain. Once out the door, she tiptoed down the narrow hall, away from the meeting room and toward a pair of closed French doors. A sign said Employees Only. She ignored it, turned the doorknob and stepped into a narrow corridor lit by flickering candles in antique brass sconces.

The second floor of a century-old house on Esplanade Avenue might be the ideal place for spirits to hang out. The atmosphere certainly fit. Creaking floorboards, dim lighting, a baroque mirror on one wall with a tiny fissure that crept from the top to the bottom of the wavy glass.

A series of doors opened off the corridor, all of them bearing a metal sign engraved with a name, all of them closed. She stopped at the first one. The sign read Quietness. Her hand curled around the doorknob, and she felt her first pang of guilt over snooping in an area that was clearly off-limits.

Then she thought of the lies Veretha and Delvin had told her when she'd called to ask about Lisa, and the guilt dissolved. She tried the door, but it was locked tight. She met the same round of bad luck with the next three doors. She could hear music coming from the door marked Serenity. Instrumental music. Haunting. Bittersweet. Somehow it reminded her of death, and she had the sudden urge to turn and run back to the room where Devlin Tishe held sway over his audience.

Spooky by design, she reminded herself as she took a deep breath and tried the knob. Surprisingly, it opened. Quietly she stepped inside and looked around as her eyes adjusted to the dimness.

Something slithered along the sofa, and her heart slammed against the walls of her chest when she realized that the movement had come from a live snake. The full-grown boa slithered to the floor, and she jumped back and into the hallway. Grabbing the doorknob, she jerked the door shut behind her, then leaned against it until her pulse slowed to a point where she could breathe without gasping.

All the talk about Devlin, but Lisa had never once mentioned a snake that looked large enough to swallow her whole. Still shaking, she crept to the next door. The sign said Awakening. This door was unlocked, as well, but she opened it slowly, afraid of what she might find. Thankfully, there was no sign of any live creatures.

The room was bathed in a soft glow, though she

couldn't see the source of the illumination. There were no overhead light fixtures. There were unlit candles, white pillars in black, wrought-iron candlesticks on either side of a pale-gray sofa.

She tiptoed to the table in the center of the room and touched her hand to the top of a glass globe the size of a beach ball that was fitted atop a pewter sculpture of a hand. As if by magic, the globe rose on a pedestal and began to revolve, catching the light and reflecting it back in glittery shimmers.

Strange, but as practical as she was, she could almost believe an evil spirit was in this room now, watching her. She shivered and turned back to the door. She'd been right about one thing. She wasn't alone.

Chapter Three

"Are you lost?" Roark's tone was accusing, his stance threatening.

Kathryn met his penetrating gaze. "I was searching for a water fountain."

He stepped toward her. "The sign on the double doors you walked through said Employees Only. Guess you missed it."

"I saw it, but I thought I heard someone back here, and I was going to ask them where I could get some water."

He leaned against the door frame. "You must have been mistaken. There's no one here except the two of us."

"So it seems." She shrugged. "Look, I made a mistake, wandered down the wrong hallway. I don't suppose you shoot people around here for that."

"Trespassing is a crime, but mistakes are usually forgiven." His face remained hard and unyielding, but his tone softened to at least a halfhearted effort toward civility. "There's water in the staff coffee area. If you'll come with me, I'll get you a glass."

"That's okay. I've quit coughing. I'll just slip back

into the meeting and listen to the rest of Mr. Tishe's lecture.''

''You'd only catch the closing statements.''

''Nonetheless, I'd like to go back.'' Kathryn started to walk away, then hesitated. ''You work for Devlin Tishe, yet I get the distinct impression that you don't want me to hear him speak. That doesn't make good business sense.''

''Ours is not an ordinary business. Devlin's message is for those seeking truth and peace.''

''What makes you think that I'm not looking for those, Mr. Lansing?''

''Perhaps the fact that you appear to be more interested in snooping than anything else.''

''I've explained and apologized. And if I weren't interested in hearing what Mr. Tishe had to say, I wouldn't be here.'' She sailed past Roark and headed down the hall.

He caught up with her and laid a hand on her arm. ''I wasn't trying to get rid of you, Kathryn. It's just that I get the feeling your expectations of us will not be realized. Devlin's doctrine is not connected with voodoo as you indicated this afternoon.''

''You set me straight. Besides, I've had unrealized expectations before. One more won't kill me.''

She pulled from his grasp and stalked toward the double doors. His next words were spoken under his breath, but they sounded a lot like ''It could.''

DEVLIN WATCHED the shapely blonde walk back into the meeting room and take the seat she'd vacated a quarter of an hour earlier. Good. He'd seen Roark follow her when she'd left. Evidently he'd persuaded her to return. Hiring Roark might well be the smartest move he'd ever made.

The man definitely had a feel for the business. Not only was the woman attractive, but she had a level of sophistication about her that suggested she had money. Money and looks, two of the attributes Devlin appreciated most in new converts. She'd make a nice addition to his group of followers.

Not that it mattered much now. With almost twelve million dollars about to be deposited in a secret bank account in the Cayman Islands, he wouldn't have to worry about a paltry five hundred here, five thousand there. Still, he'd learned long ago that nothing was a sure thing. He'd run this show until the money was in his name—unless complications developed.

Then he'd merely run. He had no intention of ever doing jail time again.

He motioned for Roark to adjust the lights and the temperature. A few closing statements before he led the audience into a chant. He scanned his listeners, making sure he was carrying them with him. He was, to a person. Even the classy blonde wore a look of intense fascination. She stood with the others as the chant began, her full sensuous hips swaying slightly with the rhythm.

Everyone was speaking in unison now, their gazes turned to him, following his lead. The sense of power surged inside him, exhilarating, pulsating deep in his soul like an aphrodisiac. This was as good as it got.

KATHRYN BREATHED a sigh of relief once the chanting was over and the formal part of the meeting was adjourned. The only thing she'd accomplished so far tonight was further proof that Devlin Tishe had his act

together, and she was certain that was what it was—
an act.

Roark Lansing was another story. He wore a sense
of danger the way he wore his shirt and jeans, provocative and seductive, almost a second skin. Lisa had
never mentioned Roark in her phone messages or her
letters, yet Kathryn was certain the two knew each
other. He was far too enigmatic to go unnoticed, even
in the presence of the charismatic Devlin Tishe.

And for some reason she couldn't quite figure out,
she was certain Roark did not want her at Mystic Isle.
Could he possibly know she was Lisa's sister? If he
did, then surely he'd share that information with Devlin, and neither would have anything to do with her.
That would leave her with no choice but to hire a new
private investigator. She probably should have done
that, anyway, but she never trusted anyone as much as
she trusted herself.

But she wasn't giving up yet. For the rest of the
evening, she planned to concentrate on Devlin Tishe,
the self-proclaimed master and the only one associated
with Mystic Isle that Lisa had mentioned by name.
Standing to the side so that a group of people could
maneuver past her, she decided to wait for the crowd
around Tishe to thin before she approached him.

Tishe saved her the trouble. He left his circle of followers and headed toward her. Their eyes met for a
second, and his look was so intimate she felt as if he'd
spanned the distance between them and physically
touched her. A few seconds later he was standing in
front of her.

She extended her right hand, but instead of shaking
it, he took it in both of his and held it. "We're honored

to have you in our midst tonight. Is this your first time with us?''

"Yes. You have a very interesting philosophy."

"It's more than a philosophy. It's truth. Spirits share the physical world with us, so why shouldn't we strive to live with them in harmony?''

"No reason that I can think of," she said, hoping to keep him talking. "I could certainly use some harmony in my life."

"And I'd love to share the full extent of my knowledge and experiences with you, Miss…''

"Richards. You can call me Kathryn."

He smiled and finally let go of her hand, letting his fingers brush hers as if he was hesitant to break the physical contact. "How did you hear about us, Kathryn?''

"I was looking in the Yellow Pages for something different to do while I was in town. Your ad seemed to speak to me.''

"Then you don't live in New Orleans?"

"No. I'm here on business."

"Hopefully you'll be in town for a long while."

"I'm not sure. I'll be here as long as it takes to complete my project." For once she was telling the truth.

"Then I hope you'll become a regular around here. We have open lectures every Tuesday night and various classes, discussion groups and personal sessions during the rest of the week.''

"I'll definitely return. I'd like to learn as much as I can about the peace you speak of.''

"I have a couple of hours free on Thursday afternoon. If your schedule permits, I'd love to meet with you privately. That way we can have an in-depth discussion.''

''That sounds great. What time?''

''How's two o'clock?''

''I'll be here.''

''Perfect.''

Kathryn looked up to see the woman in the coral skirt approaching them. She was even more attractive up close, her eyes inky black, her hair long and shiny and falling to her waist. She stopped at Devlin's side and took his arm possessively.

He patted her hand. ''Veretha, I'm glad you joined us. This is Kathryn Richards, a first-time guest.''

''Hello, Kathryn.'' Veretha's voice was smooth, honeyed. ''Welcome to Mystic Isle.''

''Thank you.''

''I'd love to stay and visit with you longer,'' Veretha said, ''but Devlin and I have a previous appointment.'' She looked up at her husband. ''Roark has already escorted Mrs. Tujacque to the Awakening Room.''

The Awakening Room, where the mood was already set and the high-tech equipment was waiting. Kathryn had the feeling that Mrs. Tujacque and a sum of money would soon be parted. But in her mind's eye, it was Lisa sitting in that room, soaking up the mysticism, falling completely under Devlin's charismatic power. So much so that she'd likely called Kathryn and asked to borrow ten thousand dollars until her trust fund came in.

The doubts surfaced in a suffocating wave. Where was Lisa now? Waiting in some hidden love nest, believing that she and Devlin and her money would escape together into some fanciful new life that didn't include Veretha? Or locked away in some cold dark chamber, held captive until she was able to purchase her release? Or was she—

No. She couldn't let her mind stray to the macabre. She needed all her wits about her. If someone was after Lisa's money, they'd surely keep her alive until it was in their hands. She had seven days to find her. And she would.

ROARK WATCHED and waited until Kathryn left the meeting room, then took the back steps two at a time. By the time she exited the building, he was already in his car with the engine running.

Kathryn stepped to the curb and looked both ways, obviously searching for a passing cab. He revved the engine, pulled up in front of her and lowered the passenger-side window.

"Do you need a lift?"

She peered through the window. "I can take a taxi."

"You might have to wait awhile. We're off the beaten path."

"Then I'll call one. I have my cell phone."

"Do I frighten you, Kathryn?"

"No. I just don't accept rides from strangers."

"I'm not a stranger. We've met twice now. But if you don't want a ride, I'll wait here until your cab comes. This isn't always the safest area after dark."

She appeared to reconsider his offer. He knew she didn't want to go with him. He also knew that she probably would.

She managed a half smile that collapsed on her almost as quickly as it appeared. "I've changed my mind. If you're certain you don't mind, I would appreciate a ride."

"If I minded, I wouldn't have offered."

She slid into the passenger seat and closed the door behind her.

He pulled into traffic. "Where to?"

"I'm staying at the Pontchartrain Hotel on St. Charles Avenue. Do you know the place?"

"I know it well."

"How long have you been with Mr. Tishe?" she asked, once she'd buckled her seat belt.

He wasn't surprised that she jumped right into the questions. After all, that was why she was in town, why she'd accepted his ride. "I've been with Devlin almost nine months."

"Really. I would have guessed years."

He swerved into the left lane to pass a slow-moving car. "What do you think of Devlin now that you've heard him speak?"

"He's unusual, but intriguing. His wife, Veretha, is, too, and very exotic."

"She's definitely that," Roark agreed. "A lot of the young guys develop serious crushes on her when they first meet her."

"Did you?" Kathryn asked.

"I wasn't that young."

"She and Devlin seem very different."

"They are. I guess it's true that opposites attract."

"Opposites," she agreed, "yet they both fit into Mystic Isle. I know you say the shop is much more than a place to buy voodoo charms, but she looks as if she could be a voodoo priestess."

So Kathryn was very perceptive, as well as intelligent and beautiful. Qualities that probably worked well for her in the business world. Qualities that could prove very dangerous if she kept hanging around Mystic Isle. He'd have to be very careful what he said around her, and yet he had to try to find a way to keep her away from Devlin.

He slowed the car and pulled into a parking place a short distance down the block from her hotel. She pushed down on the door handle, but Roark reached across the space that separated them and placed his hand on her shoulder.

"If you have any questions about Devlin or Mystic Isle, I'd be happy to try and answer them for you."

"I do have a few questions."

"Then why don't I come in and buy you a drink in the lounge?"

"I'd appreciate that."

He climbed out, walked around the car and opened her door, knowing that anything he said tonight could backfire on him. It was a chance he'd have to take.

KATHRYN LED THE WAY to a couple of empty seats at the back of the lounge, in a quiet corner where they could talk. She ordered a margarita. Roark asked for a draft.

The move from Mystic Isle to the lounge at her hotel provided a major change in atmosphere. Roark seemed less mysterious here, more like an ordinary man, but she was certain he was here for a reason, just as she was. As yet, she had no idea what his was.

"You seem to have it all together," he said, stretching his legs in front of him and leaning back in his chair.

"You make that sound like a bad thing."

"I didn't mean to. It's just that we get a lot of people like you in the shop, interested tourists checking us out, but seldom do they come back to the lectures."

"Maybe I don't have it together as much as you think. You can't always judge a book by its cover."

"Not always, but I'm pretty good at it." He stared at her as if she were a specimen under a microscope. "Why did you come back tonight?"

"I'm interested in new ideas."

"You don't work for one of those newspapers that go around the country searching for scandals to print about, do you?"

"No. If I did, would I find something?"

"Not that I know of. Devlin's authentic and a powerful persuader. He says what he believes, but he doesn't push his doctrine on anyone."

"I haven't questioned his authenticity."

"Good, because he's as honest as a preacher on his deathbed."

"That's good to know. What about you, Roark? Are you that honest?"

"I'm working on it."

As far as she was concerned, that was a totally evasive answer. But at least he was talking. "I noticed Devlin didn't ask for donations tonight," she commented, "and the lecture was free. How does he get his money?"

"He makes a lot of it from the shop. It's written up in all the tour books and frequently in national magazines and local publications. One of the cable networks even did a segment on it last year. We get at least a half-dozen tour buses stopping in most days."

"It sounds like a very lucrative business."

"It is."

"But Devlin must also get donations for his ministry."

"He does, but more on a personal level. He feels

that if he asks for open donations, people who need his services but don't have money to contribute might be hesitant to take advantage of the lectures and teaching sessions. So, he sends letters to those he feels can afford to contribute.''

''That sounds very charitable.''

''Being benevolent is part of the harmony he speaks of.'' Roark pulled some bills from his pocket and handed them to the waitress, who'd reappeared with their drinks.

She thought about the last statement. Now, Roark was trying to sell her on Devlin's considerate nature. Earlier, it seemed he'd been all but pushing her out the door. For some reason he'd changed his mind about her.

But if he was telling the truth about Devlin, then the man probably just made good business decisions. Instead of wasting his time on those with a pittance to donate, he concentrated on those with large bank accounts. And even when Lisa lived on her monthly allotment, it had been enough to let her buy nice clothes and live reasonably well. At no time in her life did she not look like a million dollars.

And at some point she'd surely have told Devlin that she was soon to do more than look like a multimillionaire. He would have fawned all over her, and her impressionable kid sister would have undoubtedly mistaken the interest in her money for love.

It made perfect sense. So where was Lisa?

''Does Devlin have satellite locations?''

''No. Mystic Isle is it. The shop and some of the offices are on the first floor. The meeting rooms are on the second, and Devlin and Veretha's private quarters are on the third floor. It's a very compact operation.''

So it seemed. She sipped her margarita. "You talk about Devlin as if he's some kind of saint. Surely he has some faults."

"All men have faults. Devlin just has a lot fewer than most of us."

She doubted that, but he probably hid them better. She had the feeling she was caught in a twisted maze where every opening led to the same dead end. Her questions were different, but the answers never seemed to get her any new information.

She set her drink on the table. Her headache was returning and fatigue was settling into her mind and body. "I hate to drink and run," she said, trying to sound nonchalant even though her concern for Lisa overrode all her emotions. "But it's been a long day and I'm fading fast."

"No problem."

He put a hand to the small of her back as they walked to the elevator. The touch was casual, yet there was no denying the increase in tension, a kind of sensual awareness that was as much mental as physical. The elevator door swung open. When she started to step inside, he pushed the button to hold the door open and took her arm, tugging her closer. "Wait."

She looked up and into his dark eyes. Still mysterious, but there was something else there, too, a depth that hadn't been there before, as if he'd dropped his facade. "What is it, Roark?"

He exhaled slowly. "I just think you should be careful, Kathryn. Be very careful."

A cold shiver shimmied along her nerve endings. "That sounds like a warning."

"It is. New Orleans is a fascinating city, but it's

dangerous, as well. And you never know where the danger may come from.''

''If there's something else I should know, Roark, please tell me.''

He shook his head. ''That's it. I just worry about a beautiful woman alone in a big city.''

But that wasn't it. He'd wanted to say more, but something had stopped him. Was it Devlin she should fear? Or was it Roark with his sensual touch and dark mysterious eyes? Or was it her questions that he and Devlin feared?

She was shaking as Roark finally moved away from the elevator and she watched the door close between them. After tonight, she was more convinced than ever that the world of Devlin Tishe was one of mystery and danger, one that had swallowed up Lisa and left no clues. She would have to be very, very careful. There was no room for mistakes. And no room for any kind of attraction to Roark Lansing.

He was on the side of the enemy.

Still, she could almost feel the pressure of his touch on her arm as the elevator climbed to the fifth floor.

December 4

THE PIERCING RING of the phone jarred Sara Ranklin from a restless sleep. She pounced on it, her pulse rate shooting skyward as she noted the time on the bedside clock. Four a.m. Calls in the wee hours of the morning were never good news, but she found them hundreds of times more frightening since Raycine had moved out of the house.

''Hello.''

''Sorry to wake you, Sara. Meant to wake Bulldog.''

It was one of the other detectives. She recognized the voice but couldn't put a name to it. "You didn't, but I will. Hold on and I'll get him for you." Her heart quit thundering and settled back in her chest. It was still probably bad news, but it was police business. It wouldn't hit so close to home.

Butch had his back to her, the sound of his rhythmic snoring filling the room. Leaning over, she put her hand on his right shoulder and shook him. He grumbled, but didn't wake up. She shook again, this time harder.

He rolled over slowly. "I wasn't snoring."

"Only enough to shake the walls, but that's not why I woke you. You have a phone call."

He grumbled and muttered under his breath, but raised himself on his elbows and took the phone from her hand. Leaving him to his conversation, she padded toward the kitchen, slowing as she passed Raycine's empty room.

Strange the way things had worked out. She'd never dreaded the empty-nest syndrome, had actually looked forward to the day when their baby left home and started college. But Raycine hadn't started college. Instead, she'd gotten involved with the wrong crowd and started spending her time partying and "hanging out" until the sun came up.

Butch had laid down the law, drawn the proverbial line in the sand. Raycine had stepped across it. That had been six months ago. During that time, they'd grown apart. Thanksgiving had come and gone without even a phone call. Now the Christmas holidays were starting, but there would be no peace or joy in their home this year.

By the time she got back to the bedroom, Butch was

pulling on a pair of jeans. "What is it this time?" she asked, stopping to watch him.

"Some fisherman getting an early start snagged a body out of Bayou St. John."

"Can't one of the other detectives take this case? You're working a half-dozen murders already."

"We all are."

"A man or a woman?"

"A woman."

"Young?"

"No word on that. So far the only one on the scene is the fisherman. That's why I need to get out there quick, before the news media and the first cops at the scene start dirtying up my crime scene."

"You never seem to get a full night's sleep anymore."

"Gotta make a living."

"You could do that just as well with a desk job."

"That's for old guys."

"Or guys who want to live long enough to get old."

"You worry too much." He kissed her on the cheek and grabbed his shoes from beside the bed. "Why don't you go back to sleep? I'll call you later."

"I will." Only she wouldn't go back to sleep and he wouldn't call her later. He never did. Once he got to the murder scene, he forgot her and everything else. He was a good husband, never fooled around on her, never treated her badly, but the job was his first love. Always had been.

DEVLIN POURED his first cup of coffee of the morning and walked to the window for a view of the city. Below him, traffic clogged the arteries leading into town. A police siren screamed over the din of other traffic noises. A typical New Orleans morning.

He loved the city and his house. It was by far the most elegant place he'd ever lived and worked. He'd miss it all when he left, but he would be going. Staying in one place for too long always led to the downfall of a good bamboozler like himself. Already the new, friendlier IRS was coming around asking questions. And sooner or later, the cops would come around, as well.

Picking up the remote control, he flicked on the TV and switched the channel so as to catch the top-of-the-hour news on the WWL Morning Show. Sally Ann was smiling at him from behind the news desk. He smiled back.

Sally Ann opened her pretty mouth and started to read from her hidden prompt. ''Local police are investigating two murders resulting from an argument outside a bar on Carollton Ave. In a separate incident, the body of a young woman was pulled from Bayou St. John near City Park. The body hasn't been identified and police...''

Hot coffee sloshed from the cup and spilled over Devlin's fingers before dripping onto his silk pajamas. He sucked in an unsteady breath. Bodies were found in New Orleans all the time. It didn't mean a thing. Not to him.

The phone shrilled and he grabbed it before it woke up Veretha. ''Good morning.''

''Devlin, I know it's early, but I need to talk to you.''

Damn. What now? He fought to hide his irritation. ''What is it, Lisa?''

Chapter Four

"I need to see you, Devlin."

"Hold on just a second." Portable phone in hand, he tiptoed to the bedroom door and peeked inside to make certain Veretha hadn't picked up the extension. Her head was half-buried beneath the covers, her breathing even. Fortunately she was a sound sleeper. Still, he took the phone out to the balcony before he resumed the conversation.

"Is something wrong, Lisa?"

"Everything's wrong. I'm bored to tears. Most of all, I miss you."

"I was out there just two days ago."

"Two days is an eternity in this place."

He understood her complaint. The rambling plantation house where she was staying was miles from the city, but it served his purposes well. For one thing the price was right. It had been in Mrs. Tujacque's family for years, empty the past twenty, prompting her to let him use it free of charge. It was also far from the eyes of the New Orleans police and anyone else who wanted to snoop into his business. Even the IRS wasn't aware that he had offices out there.

Most important Veretha hated it, which meant it provided the perfect location for his sexual indiscretions—at least it had until recently.

"I'd love to see you, Lisa, but this is a bad time. I have business I need to take care of this morning and appointments scheduled for this afternoon."

"Then send Roark to get me. He can drive me into town to meet you for lunch. Since Raycine left, I have no one to talk to."

"You have Cottonmouth and the other ladies."

"The other ladies don't like me, and Cottonmouth's no fun. I have to get out of here, Devlin, before I go crazy."

Or before she walked off on her own, the way she thought Raycine had. He couldn't afford to let that happen. "I'll see what I can do."

"Please come, Devlin. I need you."

Need. The word was like a noose, and as soon a woman said it, the noose started to tighten around his neck. He cut off the conversation as quickly as he could, but the choking sensation didn't go away.

An island in the Caribbean or some secluded seaside town in Mexico was beginning to look really good.

ROARK WIPED the vapory film from the bathroom mirror with the towel he'd just used to dry his body. Usually he slept until nine or later on his day off, but he'd awakened at seven this morning, tried to go back to sleep for half an hour, then finally got up and started the coffee. Three cups, a fully read newspaper and a shower later, he was still wrestling with the same thought.

Kathryn Morland had shown up at Mystic Isle again yesterday. She'd hung around the shop, bought a couple of books and then disappeared. If he wasn't very careful, she would undo all the work he'd accomplished in the past nine months. She'd snoop, ask questions, find out nothing, and then she'd go to the police, or worse, hire a private investigator.

Time was running out, which was why Roark should be at Tujacque's Manor today, finding some excuse to get on the computer, to look for whatever Raycine Ranklin had found the night she'd called him. The night she'd disappeared. Instead, he'd have to spend his time trying to find out exactly what Kathryn knew and what she was up to.

He knotted the towel around his waist and slathered shaving cream over his face while he considered his next move. He was fairly sure that Kathryn would see him. She wouldn't want to, but she would, just as she hadn't wanted to accept his offer of a ride two nights ago, but had, anyway.

Once the whiskers were taken care of, Roark splashed cold water on his face, blotted it dry on a clean towel and went back to the bedroom for the phone. He got the number for the hotel from information, then called and made the connection to her room.

"Kathryn Richards."

"Good morning. I hope I didn't wake you."

"You didn't. Who is this?"

So much for his making any kind of impression on her. "It's Roark Lansing." Seconds ticked away in silence. Obviously she wasn't expecting his call. "Roark, from Mystic Isle."

"Yes, I remember. Is something wrong?"

"Not unless you have a problem with an unseasonably warm day and lots of sunshine."

"No problem at all, but surely you didn't call to give me a weather report."

"Actually I called to make you an offer I hope you can't refuse."

"What kind of offer?"

"At the risk of sounding too forward, I have the day off, and I thought we might spend it together."

"Doing what?"

"Since you're interested in some of the more unusual aspects of the city, such as Mystic Isle, I thought you might enjoy a swamp tour and lunch in a neat little Cajun restaurant down the bayou. It's a chance to absorb some of the local culture and see things outside of the usual French Quarter haunts."

"I have an appointment with Devlin at two o'clock."

Damn. He should have known the guy wouldn't lose any time in checking her out, but the idea made Roark's skin crawl all the same. The man was already doing a dangerously poor balancing act with the women he had on the string, and here he was trying to pick up another.

If Devlin started investigating Kathryn, which he would if he found her at all promising, it wouldn't take him long to figure out that Kathryn Richards didn't exist.

"We could be back in plenty of time for you to keep the appointment." More silence, but at least she hadn't said no yet. "If you're not interested in that offer, we can do something else."

"No. I'd like that, if you're certain we can be back in time for my meeting with Devlin."

"As long as we get started soon. Can you be ready in half an hour?"

"Easily."

"Then I'll pick you up in front of the hotel. Wear comfortable shoes and clothes. You're not afraid of alligators, are you?"

"Isn't everybody?"

"Good point, but you won't have to tangle with them. We'll just be watching."

"Not up close and personal, I hope."

"Only if you want to. They'll be in the water. We'll be in the boat—unless you decide to go for a swim."

"Not likely."

They said their goodbyes, and Roark tugged on a pair of worn jeans and his signature black shirt. He had a closet full of them, all more or less alike. A few minutes later he'd grabbed a to-go cup of coffee and was pulling out of the parking lot of his low-rent complex. Off to row his pirogue down Baritaria Bayou with a beautiful woman along to keep him company. Beautiful and intriguing.

Damn. He'd have to watch those kinds of thoughts, be more careful than he'd been the other night at the elevator when he'd let her get to him so much that he'd almost said too much. This wasn't a date. It was part of the deadly game that pitted him against Devlin. Winner take all.

LISA PACED her second-story bedroom. She hadn't even been here a full month yet, but she knew every squeak of the floorboards, every rip in the faded wallpaper. The only good memories the room provided were the stolen hours she'd spent here with Devlin. But those were too few. The rest of the time she was left to do meaningless office tasks.

It was a far cry from the life Devlin had promised

when he'd persuaded her to give up her apartment in the city and move out to this godforsaken crumbling relic on the edge of civilization. She'd expected to see him every day, make love with him in the woods on lazy afternoons and behind the closed doors of her bedroom far into the night.

She knew it was wrong to be with him the way she wanted to be, but she loved him so much and she knew he loved her. It was just a matter of time before he'd divorce Veretha and they could be together all the time. It would happen, no matter what Roark Lansing thought. Roark was a good friend, and she appreciated his looking out for her, but he was wrong about Devlin's loving Veretha. He might have loved her once, but he didn't love her now.

She trusted Devlin, but still she missed him. She missed Raycine, too. The two of them were just beginning to bond as friends when Raycine had left without even telling her goodbye. That still hurt.

Her sister, Kathryn, must feel the same way about her, betrayed that she'd broken off all contact with her. She'd thought about that a lot lately, especially during Thanksgiving. They'd never been close in any traditional sense of the word, even though she was only three years younger than Kathryn. Even as adolescents, they'd never hung out together or talked about boys or curled each other's hair.

As adults, their relationship was frequently downright strained. Still, whenever the going got rough, Kathryn had always been there for her—lecturing, but there nonetheless.

She touched the cell phone on her waist, her one connection with the outside world. She could call, but Kathryn would demand to know where she was and what she was doing. She'd pour on the guilt, and Lisa would end up telling her everything. And, just as Devlin said, it would cause serious disharmony in both of their worlds.

Kathryn wouldn't approve of Lisa's relationship with a married man, would be certain he was only after her money, especially now that she was about to finally get her trust fund. But Devlin wasn't like that. He'd loved her even before she'd told him about the money.

In fact, he was the one who'd told her not to even call the attorney in charge of her trust fund until her birthday. They would drive up together and then they'd celebrate her being a financially liberated woman. And for her birthday he'd go with her to visit her sister, and together they'd make her understand that the love they shared was the real thing.

The hum of a car engine wafted through the open window and she yanked back the tattered curtain. It was Devlin. She'd called and he'd come. She took a quick look in the mirror, pausing to tuck long curly locks of hair behind one ear before she raced down the stairs to meet him.

DEVLIN WALKED beside Lisa, the agonizing tension he'd experienced at hearing the news of a body pulled from the bayou easing a little now that he was with her. He wasn't sure if it was her beauty or her youth that had this reassuring effect on him, or if it was just that she so openly adored him.

A breeze stirred the trees, and some of the last remaining holdouts let loose and floated down to join the dry, dead leaves already carpeting the ground. Lisa tugged him to a stop beneath an ancient oak with a knotty trunk. "I don't know why we had to come out to the woods to be together," she said. "We could have visited in my room."

"It's risky now."

"We've done it before. I'm one of your chosen ones. You told me that on Halloween night when we went through the ritual of harmony and peace."

"I know, and you're still my chosen one, my sweet Lizemera." He squeezed her hand and lifted it to his lips, kissing the tops of her fingers. "But Veretha's in one of her jealous states, and I think she may have someone following me, reporting everything I do."

"That's what I want to talk to you about, Devlin."

"Veretha's spy?"

"About my living here at Tujacque's Manor. The main reason I agreed to move out here was so that we could have more time together. Instead, I see you less."

He took her in his arms and met her gaze, trying hard to appear sympathetic. "I see you as often as I can. You know I want to see you more."

"You keep saying that, but it isn't happening."

"It will. It just takes time."

"I want to move back to town, Devlin. I want to help with the work at Mystic Isle."

He swallowed the curse that sprang to his throat. He had no time for this, no patience for nagging. "That's out of the question. I need you here."

"But that's just it, Devlin. You don't need me. You can find someone else to do what I do. My computer skills are not that good, anyway."

"But you're very good at this." He kissed her hard on the mouth, releasing his anger in the action and becoming aroused at the same time. But she didn't kiss him back, not the way she usually did. "You can't come back to Mystic Isle, Lisa. I'd love to have you close to me, but it's out of the question.''

''Because Veretha doesn't want me there?''

''She feels threatened by you.''

''She didn't seem to mind how much we were together in the beginning.''

True. She hadn't minded at all. But that was when she'd first learned about Lisa's trust fund. The Halloween ritual and the name change had been her idea, as well—stupid remnants of her previous life as a pseudo-voodoo priestess.

''I think Veretha suspects that I'm going to leave her,'' he said, trying to calm Lisa before he had to leave again.

''And you are. So why can't you just tell her about us? Why do we have to wait?''

''There's a time for everything. We must work with the spirits, move in due season.''

''You make it sound okay, but then you leave and I miss you so.'' She took his hand and placed it between her thighs. ''All of me misses you, Devlin. I'm young. I need love. I need you.''

''Just a while longer, my sweet, and then we will be together forever, in perfect harmony. Until then it's better that you stay here at Tujacque's Manor. You must trust me on this.''

He used the seductive tone and hypnotic rhythm he'd perfected for his channeling sessions. It had always worked on Lisa before, but he wasn't sure it was working today. He'd never seen her so agitated.

''I'll stay here awhile longer, Devlin, but there's something I must do.''

''What is it?''

''I want to call my sister. I won't tell her where I

am, but I've never gone this long without talking to her, and I'm sure she's worried.''

"It's not a good idea.''

"She's all the family I have. She'll never approve of you or of my being with a married man, but she does love me.''

"I'm sure she does, but I can't forget the state you were in when you first started coming to Mystic Isle. Bewildered. Wandering and searching for inner peace. You've come so far since then, grown as a person. If you talk to her now, before things are settled between us, she'll only confuse and upset you.''

"Then take me away, Devlin. Let's drive to Baton Rouge, spend the day in a hotel room making love the way we did when we first met.''

"You don't know how much I wish I could.'' He held her close, felt the heat of her body pressing into his. On another day, he might have done as she asked, run away with her for a secret tryst and a sampling of afternoon delight. But not today.

If he left with Lisa, Veretha would know in the time it took someone in Tujacque's Manor to make a phone call. And Veretha was not a woman to upset unnecessarily. She had an evil side that when she was riled, frightened even him.

He kissed Lisa again, this time getting through her wall of resistance and causing her to unleash the passion he was accustomed to. He kissed her over and over as his own blood began to pound through him, building to a crescendo that demanded release.

He stripped the clothes from her body, touched her breasts and the damp area between her legs as she writhed and moaned. With slow, sensual movements, she unzipped his trousers and stroked his arousal. After a quick look to make sure they were totally alone, he pulled her to the carpet of dry leaves. A heady sense of control shook him as they made love. The act was exciting and satisfying, though he had no fantasies about being in love with her or anyone else.

Money and power were his real mistresses, the only thing a man could truly count on.

"THERE'S ONE RIGHT over there, just off the bank."

Kathryn stared in the direction Roark was pointing. "I don't see anything."

"Just to the left of that big cypress tree."

She shaded her eyes from the sun and tried to focus. All she saw was a log—and it was moving toward them. Her heart jumped to her throat as the reptile fully surfaced, its body like rough leather, the snout long and gnarled. She'd seen hundreds of pictures of alligators, even seen the real thing at New Orleans's Audubon Zoo, but she'd never seen one slinking along the surface of a dark murky bayou just a few feet from where she was huddled in a narrow boat. "He's as long as the pirogue," she said, her voice and breathing becoming unsteady as the alligator swam closer.

"Yeah, that's a granddaddy gator. Probably close to eleven feet."

"How do you know he can't climb into the boat with us or tip us over?"

"He could—if he wanted to."

"That makes me feel so much better."

"Relax. Alligators are seldom aggressive to humans. They're looking for much smaller prey."

"And I'm smaller than you." She watched a few seconds longer, then grew even more tense as it dived beneath the surface and disappeared. "It could be anywhere," she said, looking around to be certain it wasn't crawling in the other side of the boat.

"Most likely he's on the bottom, getting away from us. We're the intruders in his world. He may not surface again for hours."

"How do you know so much about the lifestyles of bayou creatures? Are you from this area?"

"I'm from Chicago. I just find the bayou fascinating. When I'm here, I feel as if life has been reduced to its simplest form, no pretense, no false facades. Just water and earth, plant and animal, predator and prey."

She stared at Roark and had trouble seeing him as the man she'd met in Mystic Isle three days ago. He had the same dark eyes that burned with intensity when he looked at her, the same intriguing quality to his voice, the same thick dark hair that never stayed in place. The same hard lines of muscle and bronzed flesh. The same raw sensual appeal that left her weak.

So maybe he wasn't different at all. Perhaps it was Mystic Isle that provided the mysticism. Or maybe she was being sucked in the same way Lisa had been sucked into the world of spirits and unseen powers. There was no denying that in spite of everything, she'd enjoyed being with him today. Liked seeing the ripple of his muscles as he rowed the boat. Liked the way he fit into this world of quiet understated mystery as well as he did into the fake intrigue of Mystic Isle.

But she didn't trust her feelings. "Why did you really ask me out here today, Roark?"

"To spend time with you. I like your company." He laid the oars inside the boat and met her gaze. "Why did you come?"

"Do you always answer questions with questions?"

"I answered your question. It was you who didn't answer mine."

"I'm not sure why I came," she lied. "Or why you'd want to spend time with me."

"Why wouldn't I?"

"See, there you go with the questions again."

"Okay, you're a smart, very attractive, no-nonsense, self-assured woman who knows where she's going and what she wants from life. I find that fascinating."

"And I suppose you get that from some sort of aura I put off?"

"Your personality is painted into your aura. You're surrounded by a halo of light with flecks of gold. But I also read your personality in your walk, the tilt of your head, the way you look right at me when we talk. The way you pushed your way right past doors marked Private. You're used to going after what you want."

"So you see me as some attractive but cold, calculating bitch?"

"I don't see you as cold. Under the right circumstances, I imagine you can be incredibly hot, passionate and fiery, and I definitely don't see you as a bitch."

The talk of fire and heated passion seemed to dip inside her, stir some sensual, erogenous area connected more to her mind and soul than her body. Or maybe it was the man sitting so close to her that stirred those feelings. She didn't trust him, yet there was no way to be around him without being aware of him as a rugged, extremely virile man.

She'd never believed in auras, seldom believed in anything she couldn't back up with facts, but Roark did affect her senses in strange ways. Perhaps that was the effect of *his* aura, or else she was just reacting to sheer sexual arousal, a weakness she hadn't succumbed to in a very long time.

"Were you searching for yourself when you discovered Devlin's teachings?" she asked, changing the subject to one that would keep her on her self-appointed task.

"I was searching for money to buy my next whiskey. Fortunately a friend introduced me to Devlin, instead of buying me a drink. But I have found myself since uniting with him. I owe him a lot."

Roark picked up the oars again, sank them into the water and began the rhythmic rowing motion that let the boat slide across the surface of the bayou. "I say we drop the subject of Devlin and have lunch."

She looked around. Tall cypress trees and giant clusters of palmetto lined the bank, and the low areas were filled with murky water. As far as she could tell, the whole area was a breeding ground for the alligators, nutria, turtles and snakes Roark had pointed out to her on their ride through the bayou. Her stomach twisted, reneging at the thought of joining the swamp creatures. "Where would we eat?"

"There's a small restaurant around the next bend."

"Out here in the middle of nowhere?"

"Trust me. It's there."

"Can I trust you, Roark Lansing?"

He captured her with his gaze, dark, penetrating, mesmerizing. "Sometimes it's better to trust no one, Kathryn. But I'm not going to hurt you, at least not intentionally. That's the one thing you can be sure of."

And suddenly she wanted desperately to trust him, to just blurt out the question that walked through her mind by day and screamed in her dreams by night.

Where is my sister? Where is Lisa Morland? She wanted to, but she didn't trust him that much.

He eased the boat to the bank, poling it up on the muddy earth, through thick clusters of water hyacinths and between an army of cypress knees.

He climbed from the boat and took her hand. A tremble shot through her body, an awareness so intense she lost her balance as she stepped from the boat. He caught her and pulled her close, holding her steady. When she looked up, her face was mere inches from his.

And she knew he was going to kiss her.

Chapter Five

Roark's arms tightened around Kathryn, desire hitting so quickly and with such a wallop, he had no time to prepare for the onslaught. Her lips were full, sensuous, waiting. He met her gaze, and the ache inside him swelled to a painful lump in his chest.

The hunger took over, an urge so powerful it addled his brain, making it almost impossible to do what it had to do. Still, with muscles tight as spring-wound cords, he released his hold on her and backed away.

He watched her take a deep breath and turn away from him. He'd won the battle, but it provided little satisfaction. Instead, he felt less a man than he had in a long time, as if he'd lost part of himself during the nine months he'd worked so closely with Devlin and Veretha. Nonetheless, he had his own agenda, and he couldn't let anyone or anything sabotage it.

STILL SHAKEN from the near kiss, Kathryn followed Roark across the marshland, sticking to the worn path and the high ground the way he did to avoid stepping into pits of muddy slush.

His behavior puzzled her as much as her own did. She wasn't used to feeling the kind of sudden and unbridled physical attraction she'd experienced with him almost from the moment they'd met.

And she wasn't used to a man pulling away from a kiss that was all but in progress. The fact that he had only added to her conviction that he had something to hide.

She'd have to play her part in this charade as well as Roark did if she wanted to get any information from him. Appear gullible, impressionable, genuinely taken with the mysticism he and Devlin worked so hard to create.

Actually she'd probably started a few minutes ago when she'd gone weak at Roark's touch. That time the emotions had been genuine. The next time they wouldn't be. She was not a slow learner.

The restaurant was little more than a shack, but the odors emanating from it had Kathryn's mouth watering even before they reached the parking lot. From the water she'd thought they were miles from any civilization. Looks had been deceiving. A blacktop road ran right in front of the restaurant, and a big sign welcomed the hungry to Yvonne's for the best Cajun food in Louisiana.

It might be more truth than bragging. At least a dozen vehicles were parked in the lot, even though it was only five past eleven.

"How did you ever find this place?" she asked as they rounded a pickup truck with a gun rack and two rifles hanging in the back window.

"Veretha brought me down here. She's the one who introduced me to the bayou country."

Roark and Veretha. Perhaps the two of them had a thing going. That was a possibility she hadn't considered, but it didn't seem far-fetched at all after hearing her sister talk about Devlin the way she had.

"You and Veretha must be good friends."

"Everyone who gets involved with Mystic Isle becomes friends. It's part of the spirit of unity that exists among us."

Yeah, right. The unity and harmony Lisa had spoken of sounded more like adultery, now that Kathryn knew Devlin had a wife. The relationship between Roark and Veretha could easily be the same flavor.

"Knowing you always have friends to count on must be very comforting," she said, working hard at playing gullible. "Veretha must get around. This is a long way from Mystic Isle."

"She has many interests."

Like voodoo and curses. And Roark.

"Hope you're hungry," he said, breaking into her thoughts. "There's not a lot of variety, but everything Yvonne cooks is delicious, that is, if you like spicy fare."

"If it's delicious, I can handle it."

Roark opened the door and she stepped inside. She looked around as her eyes adjusted to the cozy dimness. The floor was bare wood planks, the tables mismatched and covered in white butcher paper, the ceilings low. Talk and laughter reverberated through the narrow, oblong dining area.

A petite young waitress with long dark lashes and huge expressive eyes spotted them and smiled shyly as she walked toward them. "You keep away too long, Roark. You forget your way down the bayou?"

"I didn't forget. Just not a lot of time for fishing lately."

"Veretha comes often."

"Really? When was she here last?"

"Four nights ago."

"Was she alone?"

"No. A man, he come with her. Not Mr. Devlin."

"She has lots of friends in the area."

"I never seen this friend before. He's not one of us."

Roark nodded but didn't respond to the comment. "We'll take the table in the back," he said, tilting his head toward one in the far corner, away from the crowd. Kathryn didn't miss the flash of jealousy in the young woman's eyes.

"Is that Yvonne?" she asked as he held her chair.

"It's her daughter, Michelle. I'm sure Yvonne is in the kitchen, making sure everything's done right."

"Michelle likes you."

"A girlish crush."

"She's not so young, and she looks at you with a woman's eyes—not a girl's."

He took the chair across from her. "There's nothing between Michelle and me, if that's what you're thinking."

"I was just making an observation. You don't have to explain your relationships to me."

"If I did, it would be a short conversation."

She doubted that, but whatever he did apart from his involvement with Devlin was none of her business, and she planned to keep it that way. She scooted her chair closer to the table. "We didn't get menus."

"That's because there aren't any. When they got so stained from hot sauce and beer you couldn't read them anymore, Yvonne trashed them and never bothered to have new ones printed."

"So how do you know what to order?"

"There's usually a few specials printed on the board

over the bar." He motioned in that direction. "And there's always seafood gumbo, potato salad, fried oysters, shrimp and catfish—with lots of beer or iced tea to wash it down. And bread pudding floating in rum sauce for dessert."

Suddenly she was famished. "I'll take one of each."

"Good. I like a woman with an appetite."

She scanned the specials on the board. Flounder, topped with crabmeat and shrimp. Soft-shell crab platter. Chicken and *andouille* gumbo. *"Andouille."* She let the word roll off her tongue, playing with the pronunciation. "What is that and how do you say it?"

"The *l*'s are silent, so it's just ahn-dewey. It's a pork sausage, highly seasoned with peppers, herbs and spices. Good for the taste buds and for developing ulcers."

"Think I'll pass on that. What are you having?"

"A soft-shell crab po-boy," he said, as if the choice were a given.

She glanced back at the board. "It doesn't say the crab comes as a po-boy."

"Everything comes as a po-boy. Yvonne makes her own bread, crusty on the outside, light and fluffy on the inside. It's as good as you'll find anywhere." He took a cellophane-wrapped package of crackers from a small basket on the table. "Have you tried soft-shell crab before?" he asked as he ripped the plastic from the crackers.

"No, but I've seen them on other people's plates. They have little legs sticking out."

"Terrific, crispy little legs. I recommend them."

She was tempted, but not convinced. When Michelle came to take their order, she went with a shrimp po-boy. She was surrounded by the strange and unfamiliar.

The least she could do was eat something she'd tried before.

A minute later Michelle returned with iced tea for both of them, condensation dripping from the tall glasses and sliding onto the paper napkin that served as a coaster. Kathryn sipped her tea, cognizant of the cold as it attacked her fingertips, aware of Roark's constant gaze. Tension hovered between them in spite of the relaxed setting and his earlier attempt at casual conversation.

"This is an interesting place," she said, trying to keep her tone light. "Is taking new visitors to Mystic Isle out for swamp tours and lunch in your job description?"

"It comes under the category of 'Other duties as needed.' So I only take the ones who fascinate me."

"How many would that be—one a week, three a month? Just a ballpark figure."

"Let's see. I've been here nine months…. So, I guess that would be one every nine months. Just a ballpark figure."

"Why me?"

"Like I said, you fascinate me." He stretched his arms across the table and placed his hands over hers.

Her heart jumped, then settled painfully in her chest. In spite of her resolve not to feel anything for him, she'd reacted to his touch as if it had been sparked by electricity. She pulled her hands away and tucked them safely in her lap. "Tell me about Devlin Tishe."

His facial expression changed, the muscles tightened, and his eyes took on a shadow of suspicion. She'd have to step easy, keep it light. "He's very impressive," she added. "I liked hearing him talk."

"Most people do." Roark unrolled his paper napkin,

removed the silverware and lined it up on his left. "He's a powerful speaker, but he's also a genuinely nice guy."

Yeah, and some people probably said that about Jack the Ripper. "I'd think a man like Devlin would have some special place to train his followers."

"You mean like a school?"

"Kind of like that. Maybe a place where they could stay and be with others who believed the same way."

"Ah, you mean like a commune." Roark rolled his eyes, as if she'd suggested something preposterous. "This is the new millennium, Kathryn, and Devlin is a very modern man. He wouldn't shut himself away from the world, and he definitely wouldn't expect anyone else to. He gives lectures, classes and private sessions, all in his headquarters above the shop. He shares a doctrine. He doesn't lead a cult."

Michelle appeared at his elbow with their food. "Mama give you the biggest crab in the kitchen," she said, placing Roark's plate in front of him.

"Tell your mama I appreciate it."

He smiled, and Kathryn couldn't help but notice how it eased the lines in his forehead and formed gentle creases around the corners of his eyes, making him look almost boyish and not nearly as mysterious as he did when he studied her so intently.

"Apparently Yvonne is taken with you, too," she teased when Michelle walked away and left them to their food.

"I did her a favor once. She never forgets." He lifted the top slice of bread and shook on a few more drops of hot sauce.

"What kind of favor?"

"Nothing much, but she's a good Cajun woman.

You take care of her, she takes care of you.'' A gob of tartar sauce squeezed from between the thick slices of bread and fell back onto the plate when he lifted the sandwich. He took a huge bite, ending the conversation without satisfying her curiosity about the favor.

She followed suit, squeezing her own overstuffed sandwich so that it would fit into her mouth. Roark had told the truth about at least one thing. The food at Yvonne's was delicious. She dropped her questions and savored the taste.

Roark had almost finished his lunch when his cell phone rang. He answered it, then excused himself from the table and went outside to continue the conversation. Apparently the call was not good news. He came back shortly, but never took another bite of the sandwich he'd been devouring minutes earlier.

The trip back to New Orleans was strained and mostly silent until he pulled up in front of the hotel. Then from out of the blue, he reached across the car seat and took her hand. ''I'd like to ask an unusual favor of you, Kathryn.''

She looked into his eyes and saw nothing but a stony glaze, as if their penetrating depths had been drained dry. Anger, skepticism, mistrust. They'd all surfaced from time to time on the ride home, but they were swallowed up now in a swell of apprehension.

''What is it, Roark?''

''I'd appreciate it if you didn't mention to Devlin or Veretha that we were together today.''

''Why would that matter?''

''It's a long story. I can't go into it now. You don't have to lie. Just leave me and anything we talked about last night and today out of the conversation. Will you do that for me?''

"Can't you give me a reason why I should?"

He squeezed her hand, and an involuntary shudder skittered up her backbone and gave her chills. She didn't know him. He didn't know her. And yet she felt as if she'd been drawn into some conspiracy with him.

"I can't go into it now, but it's important."

Important how? To whom? The questions dogged her mind. "I can't promise anything, Roark, but I won't mention it unless I feel it's necessary."

"Then I guess I'll have to settle for that."

She started to climb out of the car, then hesitated. "Will I see you again?"

"You know where to find me."

"Will I see you away from Mystic Isle?"

"Do you want to?"

"Yes." For all the right reasons. And for all the wrong ones.

"I'll call you. Take care, Kathryn." Before she could respond, he leaned across the seat and touched his lips to hers. The kiss was quick, yet so intense she was shaking as she stepped onto the curb.

By the time she'd stepped into the opulent warmth of the hotel lobby, a nagging doubt had replaced the temporary elation. Roark had resisted the urge to kiss her in the swamp. Yet he hadn't hesitated when he'd needed a favor. She had to be stronger, see past his darkly seductive powers and never forget why she was here. Roark was a means to an end, one of the keys to unlocking the mystery of Devlin Tishe and Mystic Isle.

An oak-shrouded mansion of locked doors and communing with spirits. A shop full of curses and spells and carved vipers that seemed alive. A world that Lisa had embraced so completely that she'd cut off all contact with the only family she had.

And now Lisa had vanished into the thick, choking humidity of a city that hugged the crescent of a murky river and clung to its past like a child groping a cheap string of Mardi Gras beads.

A minute ago Kathryn had felt inexplicably connected with Roark. But like everything else in his world, it was only an illusion. The truth was, she had never been more alone.

DEVLIN SAT in his leather swivel chair, so shaken he could barely speak coherently. But he had to hold it together, conceal the alarm that seethed just below the mask of composure he'd perfected years ago. Grief was okay at a time like this. Panic was out of the question.

"I appreciate your getting here so fast, Roark."

"I could tell how upset you were on the phone. What's happened?"

"A woman's body was dragged out of Bayou St. John in the wee hours of the morning." He cradled his forehead in his palms, then dropped his hands to his lap and exhaled sharply. "I just heard on the noon news that the body had been identified. It was Raycine Ranklin."

"Son of a bitch," Roark muttered, then strode to the window and stared outside, his hands knotted into hard fists. When he turned back around to face Devlin, every line in his face was drawn.

"What happened?"

"The only thing they said on the news was that there was evidence of foul play."

Roark stared at him, his eyes unreadable.

"I didn't kill her, Roark."

"I never suspected that you did."

Devlin breathed a little easier. He should have

known Roark would never doubt him. He was one of the few he could always count on. "I appreciate that, Roark. I'm not sure Detective Ranklin will feel the same way."

"Have you talked to him?"

"Not yet, though I expect he'll come calling soon."

"From what Raycine told me, she'd never mentioned the fact that she was involved with us to either of her parents. She was certain they wouldn't approve."

A notion that Devlin had planted in her mind. He'd warned her never to tell them that she was coming to Mystic Isle and definitely never to mention that she was living at Tujacque's Manor and working for him. Her father would have understood what was going on all too well. Butch Ranklin knew the score.

"It's not her family I'm worried about," Devlin said. "It's that riffraff she hung out with in the French Quarter before she found us and came into the truth."

"I doubt any of that group will talk to Ranklin or any other cop."

"I'm not so sure. I remember one of them who came here a few times asking about Raycine. A homeless gutter punk with the mouth of a drunken sailor." Devlin swung his chair to the left so that he could watch Roark's expression, make sure he was getting through to him. "Anyway, just in case Ranklin comes around, I think we should have our story straight."

"What story is that, Devlin?"

"Raycine came to a few meetings here, then seemed to lose interest. She was a nice young woman, but clearly disturbed. We haven't seen her in a couple of months."

"Two months ago was when she moved into Tujacques Manor."

"Exactly. After that, no one saw her around here, so no one can dispute our story. It's not that I want to lie, Roark. But you know Ranklin's nickname."

"Raycine said the guys on the force call him Bulldog."

"Exactly. If the man comes in here harassing our flock, he'll get everybody nervous, cause serious disharmony among our group. There's no reason to let this happen when we know that no one here had anything to do with Raycine's death."

Roark continued to stare out the window, sunlight sliding through the blinds and painting his face in stripes of light and shadow. For all the emotion that showed on his face or in his stance now, the man could have been a lifeless stone statue. Roark was tough as steel. Devlin was lucky to have him on his side.

Finally Roark turned to face him. "Did they say how long the body had been in the water?"

"Like I said, they gave no details."

Roark crossed the room toward the door. "A week ago she was inside the fold. Now she's dead."

"I think she may have been running from someone when she came to us. I guess when she went back to the streets, the trouble caught up with her."

"It's just too bad," Roark said, the strain in his voice indicating he was not the statue he seemed. "She had a lot of good inside her." He opened the door.

Devlin stood. "There is one other thing before you go."

"What's that?"

"I don't want Lisa to find out about this."

"She'll find out, all right, and soon. When the

daughter of a NOPD detective gets killed, it's big news.''

"She won't find out as long as she doesn't leave the plantation house. There's only one television set there and no radios. I've told Cottonmouth to disconnect a few wires in the TV and to tell Lisa that it's broken.''

"I forget that Tujacques is so totally isolated from the rest of the world.''

"Lisa has been chosen by the spirits, Roark, as Raycine had been. She needs time away from the stress and disharmony of the world so that she can grow in knowledge and power.''

"Yeah. I guess Raycine needed a little more time.''

"If she'd stayed with us, she'd still be alive. That's why I don't want Lisa to find out about this. She and Raycine had become good friends and she's not strong enough yet to handle such devastating news. I've contacted the cellular-phone service company. They're going to restrict the service on her phone to a few select numbers.''

"Who will she be able to call, besides you, of course?''

"Mystic Isle extensions and your cellular number.''

"What did she say when you told her that?''

"I didn't tell her. Those are the only people she calls, anyway, so I doubt she'll even notice the restriction for a while. By then I may feel she's strong enough to handle the truth.''

"Sounds as if you've taken care of everything.''

"I have to. So many people depend on me, and I don't want to let them down. So if Detective Ranklin calls you, you don't know a thing about Raycine, haven't seen or heard from her since the end of September.''

"Raycine who?"

"That's what I want to hear." Devlin straightened his tie and plucked the jacket of his slate-gray Armani suit from the back of his chair. Thankfully, Kathryn Richards would be here any minute.

He'd never needed a diversion more.

ROARK TOOK the steps rather than the elevator back to the first floor. Devlin's demeanor hadn't fooled him for a minute. The man was running scared, and probably with good reason. The word on the street was that Butch Ranklin earned his nickname, that when he went after a man, he did it with his teeth bared and his guns blazing. He was a dead-or-alive kind of cop.

Devlin knew that, and still he'd taken Raycine into his inner circle, moved her out to Tujacque's Manor and put her to work. He'd said it was because she had nowhere else to go, but Roark had never known Devlin to make any sacrifice for the dozens of other homeless people who wandered in off the street to hear his lectures—not unless that person had something Devlin needed or wanted.

Raycine had both. Not only was she an impressionable beauty who was thrilled by his attention, but she was an extremely talented computer hacker. She could learn more about a person in thirty minutes on the Internet than some private investigators could learn in a month. She knew where the subject shopped, what he spent, what his passions were, who he'd slept with and where, and most important, his level of income.

Still, it had been risky for Devlin to go after a woman whose father wore a badge. Roark had warned him. He hadn't wanted police interference any more than Devlin did. But the man had ignored his advice, let the sense of power lead him into a major mistake.

The heat was on now—for all of them. If Roark didn't move fast, he'd be forced to spend the rest of his life knowing he'd blown his chance to settle a long-standing score with Devlin Tishe. He had to spend more time at the old plantation house, find a reason to go out there and an opportunity to get on the computer. The information was there. He just had to find it.

By the time he made it downstairs, Kathryn was walking through the door, dressed to kill in an olive-colored sweater that hugged the swell of her breasts and a pair of tailored black slacks.

"That was a quick change," he said, aching to say more, to warn her to run like hell and not to stop until she was far away from everything connected to Mystic Isle.

"Do you like it?" she said, turning to show off the full effect of her outfit.

"You look great, but then, you looked great in your jeans and sweatshirt."

"Thanks."

"Devlin's waiting for you in his office."

"Then I guess there's no reason to keep him waiting."

"None that I can think of," he said as she walked past him. No reason at all—unless she wanted to live.

Chapter Six

Roark's thumbs raked across the tops of the manilla folders, checking the name on each one as he passed it. Ran, Ras, Rat—no Ranklin. If Devlin had kept any information on Raycine in the low-security files at Mystic Isle, he'd pulled it. Of course, that didn't mean they'd been destroyed. A man like Devlin always kept records, proof of what he'd gotten away with.

The problem for Roark was laying his hands on those records. Whether in hard or soft copy, they were likely carefully locked away from scrutiny, most likely at the plantation house, miles from Mystic Isle.

And admission to Tujacque's Manor was by invitation only, and no one but Devlin or Veretha had the authority to issue that invitation. Roark had been out there on many occasions, usually to accompany Devlin or to deliver or pick up something. But Cottonmouth had always been there, in the background, saying little, but watching everything.

Cottonmouth was a giant of a man with thighs the size of tree trunks. In his midfifties, the guy was still fit as a heavyweight boxer. Strong body, weak mind. He'd lost a lot of his reasoning power to a drug addiction that had almost put him in the grave. He was convinced that Devlin had not only saved him from an agonizing death but had contacted the spirit of his daughter, who'd died from an overdose, and made everything right between the two of them.

Other than Cottonmouth, Lisa was the only person who actually lived on the premises. Before Lisa had moved out there, there had been several young women who lived and supposedly worked at the plantation house, though Roark never saw evidence of much work, other than flyers they'd typed and copies they'd made, tasks that could have easily been done at Mystic Isle.

As far as Roark could determine, Raycine was the first one who'd actually performed a service other than cater to Devlin's physical needs. That was why she'd been allowed to stay on when Lisa, or Lizemera as she was called now, had been moved to the crumbling estate.

Lisa and her trust fund were the plum of a lifetime, and Devlin was not stupid enough to lose his chance at it by making Lisa jealous. Devlin had no clue that Roark knew about the trust fund. But then, there was a lot Devlin didn't know about Roark Lansing.

"So here you are. I've been looking all over for you."

He stiffened as Veretha's voice coiled around him, the sulky, breathless quality seeming to suck the air from the room. She walked up behind him and slid her arms around his waist, touching her lips to the back of his neck.

"You know you shouldn't do that here. Someone could see you."

"What does it matter?"

He stepped away from her, then turned to meet her

entreating gaze. "You're married to my boss, remember?"

"Why should I remember? He never does."

"You know that's not true. He's devoted to you."

She drew her full red lips into a pout. "So devoted he left this morning without even telling me goodbye."

"I'm sure he had his reasons."

"He did. Lisa called and he went running."

"Did he tell you that?"

"He doesn't have to tell me. I have my ways." She propped on the edge of a low table, crossed her legs and swung one seductively. "You've been working here for nine months, Roark. Don't you think it's time we get to know each other better?"

"We already know each other well."

"Not as well as I'd like." She hitched her skirt up a few inches, revealing a lot more leg than he needed to see, then curled her tongue over her lips, moistening them. "Do I make you hot, Roark?"

"You make me nervous."

"Good."

"Not good, Veretha. Devlin's not only my boss, he's my friend."

"Then you know that he has his needs and his own ways of satisfying them. But I have my needs, too, Roark, and I'm tired of being left alone in my bed while he runs to Lisa's."

"In that case you can have any man you want, Veretha. You don't need me."

"But you're the man I want."

"What about the guy you took to Yvonne's the other night?"

"Johnny? He's just a friend. How do you know about that?"

"I had lunch at Yvonne's. Her daughter mentioned you'd been in."

"Michelle talks too much. She should tend to her own business." She slid her hands between the hair at the back of her neck, lifted the shiny black locks to the top of her head, then let them fall down her back, so long they reached past her waist. She tossed her head so that the last of the flyaway strands slid away from her eyes.

"Is Johnny a friend from your previous life?" Roark asked, ignoring the move he was certain was designed to affect his libido.

"Don't sound so accusing. Those are my friends. I can't just abandon them."

"If Devlin finds out what you're doing down in the bayou country, he's not going to like it."

"So what will he do? Leave me for Lisa Morland? He's probably already thinking about that."

"He'd never leave you."

"You're so trusting, Roark. That's what I like about you. That and your gorgeous body." She slid from the table and walked toward him, the silky skirt clinging to her swaying hips. "Kiss me."

He swallowed hard. "I could never be satisfied with just a kiss, Veretha. If we went that far, I'd want more. I'd want all of you."

"Then take me." Her painted nails caught the spaghetti straps of her blouse and pulled them from her shoulders. "I'm all yours."

"Not here. Not now." He struggled to find an excuse she'd buy without feeling scorned. The last thing he needed was her fury. He glanced at his watch. "I have a meeting scheduled with Devlin at three-thirty. It's almost that now."

Her hands flew to her hips and fire danced in her eyes. "Devlin. Always Devlin."

"Not always, Veretha. One day it will be me." He sincerely hoped that was true, only he didn't mean it the way it sounded. He had no interest at all in Veretha except as a means to the desired end.

She sighed and backed away from him. "Monday night, Roark. I want you with me when I go back to the bayou country."

"I don't think you should go. You're not a voodoo priestess any longer. You're Devlin's wife."

"Once a priestess, always a priestess."

"That's not what I hear. You're only a true priestess if you follow the prescribed teachings and rituals."

"I make my own rituals. I don't need Devlin's approval for what I do, and I don't need anyone else's. You've been down the bayou with me before. They love me."

"Give it a rest, Veretha. This is no time for you to go making waves. No trips down the bayou. No snakes. No trouble."

"Monday night, Roark. It's all arranged. I will go and I want you with me."

She didn't wait for an answer. It was more an order than a request, anyway. Only, this time he might have to refuse. He didn't have time to waste on her wild excursions into mystical and dangerous rituals. His chances were slipping away so quickly, rushing like the tides going back to sea. If he missed the opportunity to act, it would never come again.

One chance to make Devlin Tishe pay for stealing the only person he'd ever loved who'd loved him back, completely, unconditionally, the way love was supposed to be. He'd made mistakes, and he'd paid for them a million times over. Now it was Devlin's time to pay. That was why Roark had thrown out all the rules, why he'd do whatever he had to do, any way he had to do it.

Even if it meant drawing Lisa and Kathryn into the sticky, dangerous web. For a second he was back at the bayou and Kathryn was in his arms, her lips ready and waiting. The need to kiss her rocked through him again, the same way it had this morning, powerful, all-consuming.

He slammed his right fist into his left palm, an unsuccessful attempt to release his frustration. He'd never meant it to come to this, had never thought he'd put anyone in danger but himself. But he should have known. His life had been a lesson in the fact that when all hell broke loose, it would take no prisoners.

KATHRYN STOOD by the door to Devlin's office, ready to go but disappointed that she'd spent an hour with him and learned nothing that would help in her search. The time had flown by, though. He was every bit as charming and as mesmerizing as Lisa had said.

"I'm glad you came in today, Kathryn. Talking to you has been good for me. You're like a breath of fresh air."

"I can't be that different from the other women who come to Mystic Isle."

"But you are. They usually require so much from me that I feel drained when they leave. I feel that you gave me at least as much as I gave you."

"I gave you nothing."

"But you did," he whispered, his tone intimate. "You are witty and intelligent, and you seem so open to new ideas. I know that we will do well together. You have such a capacity for love and harmony.''

"Only if I learn it from someone as knowledgeable as you.''

"Then we'll make sure that happens.'' He took both her hands in his. "I think we should start tomorrow night. One of my dear friends, Grace Tujacque, is having a party, and I'd love for you to go with us.''

This was just the opportunity she was looking for, yet dread crawled around inside her like spiders in search of prey. He was talking to her, yet she imagined him saying the same words to Lisa.

He'd sucked Lisa in with his charisma and seductive powers, and while she stood here talking to him, listening to his polished lines, he could be holding her sister prisoner somewhere. Either that or he had her so brainwashed that she was willingly under his command and influence, just waiting until the day she could collect her inheritance and turn it over to him.

The possibilities were frightening. But at least in those possibilities, Lisa was alive. Kathryn had to hold on to that hope now, had to believe that even though Lisa had seemingly dropped from the face of the earth, she was alive.

"You seem hesitant,'' Devlin said, letting go of her hands. "It was only a suggestion. I'll certainly understand if you say no. I'll be disappointed, but not angry.''

"What would Veretha say about my going to the party as your guest?''

"So that's what's bothering you. You needn't worry. I think you've met Roark Lansing. I'll invite him, as well, make it a foursome. Will that ease your worries?''

"In that case, I'd love to go to the party.''

Devlin reached for the phone on his desk. "Let me find someone to drive you back to your hotel."

"That won't be necessary. I can take a taxi." But he'd punched in an extension before the words were out of her mouth. A few seconds later he returned the receiver to its cradle. "It's all taken care of. Roark is waiting for you inside the shop. It will give you a chance to get to know him better."

"That's very considerate, but I really could have taken a taxi back to the hotel."

"Nonsense." Devlin walked with her to the elevator, his hand at the small of her back, as if they were old friends or more. "I'll pick you up tomorrow night at eight. May the spirits guide and protect you until we're together again," he crooned as he trailed a finger down her right arm. The touch was far too intimate, and she had to fight an unexpected shudder as she stepped onto the elevator.

People, voices, smells, sounds. Everything inside Mystic Isle was surreal. She couldn't wait to leave this place, to feel the heat of the sun and the sting of the wind. Only how much escape could there be with Roark sitting beside her in the car?

Two men, both part of this mystical, mysterious world, yet one filled her with a sickening dread and the other held some insane, inexplicable attraction. But one thing was certain—neither of them could be trusted.

THE COLD BLACK SNAKE slithered and curled about Veretha's right arm as she watched Roark pull away from the curb with the pretty blonde she'd met last night sitting beside him. But it wasn't Roark the woman had come to see. It was Devlin.

She'd known from the beginning that Devlin's sexual appetite was as ravenous and twisted as his desire for wealth. She'd been a fool to think she could satisfy him, to believe his lies that the others were only playthings, that he loved no one but her. The bitter truth was that he loved only himself.

And now that Raycine's body had been discovered, the pressure would escalate. She could just wake up one morning and find him gone, not to the ratty old plantation house where he'd gone this morning, but gone for good, him and millions of dollars.

That could well be the way Devlin planned it. But that was not the way it would happen. She may have been a fool in the past, but she wasn't one now.

She'd pulled herself up from the ghettos of New Orleans and created a following for herself long before she'd gotten entangled with Devlin, and she would not be bested by a depraved con man. She'd see both him and Lisa dead first. As dead as the nosy Raycine Ranklin was.

Closing her eyes, Veretha ran her hands along the smooth cold body of the snake. Her days of playing the loving wife and forsaking the curses and charms that gave her power over her enemies were over. She was *Veretha,* the true chosen one.

She loved Devlin, loved him more than she'd ever thought it possible to love any man. But she'd had enough. She could find happiness with someone else if it came down to that, someone young and virile, like Roark. He might not want her now, but he'd want her if she had Lisa's millions.

Devlin would see things her way. Or he'd see them from the other side, with the spirits he claimed to know so well.

ST. CHARLES AVENUE was bustling with activity by the time Roark pulled up in front of Kathryn's hotel. Traffic along the famed, oak-canopied avenue was heavy, and a noisy group of teenagers in school uniforms were waiting at the streetcar stop, their shoulders drooped from the weight of their book bags. A couple of skimpily clad college-age women jogged down the neutral ground, and an elderly man was being walked by a golden retriever tethered to a leash.

On a normal visit to New Orleans, Kathryn would have found the scene fascinating. Today she saw it only as a backdrop for the bizarre turn her own life had taken in the past twenty-four hours. Trying to hold on to the logic of the real world, she was obsessed with delving into the depths of the one inhabited by Roark, Devlin, Veretha and the unseen spirits of good and evil.

Roark had seemed preoccupied during the drive back to the hotel, barely talking, remaining cool and aloof. Very different from the amiable man who'd taken her boating down a secluded bayou and bought her lunch at an intriguing Cajun restaurant.

"Thanks for the ride," she said.

Finally he turned and met her gaze. "You can thank Devlin when you see him again. He's the one who arranged for the lift."

The bellman walked to the car and opened the door for her. She nodded an acknowledgment, but made no move to get out. The bellman got the message and walked away. She turned back to Roark. "Have I done something to upset you?"

"I don't know. Have you?"

"I didn't tell Devlin anything about our being together this morning."

"Then you haven't upset me."

"Well, something has. Your attitude has definitely changed since this morning."

He exhaled slowly and shrugged. "I'm sorry. It wasn't intentional. I just have a lot on my mind."

"I'm a good listener if you'd like to talk."

"Maybe another time."

"Then I guess it's goodbye for now." Only, she didn't want him to leave, hated the thought of being alone right now. "What will you do for the rest of the afternoon?"

"Probably go back to Mystic Isle."

"On your day off? It's much too nice to stay inside."

He rolled the palm of his hand around the steering wheel. "I'm guessing you have a suggestion."

"I could use some exercise. It's always nicer to walk with company."

He nodded. "Most things are more fun with the right company."

"So is that a yes or a no?"

"It's a yes, as long as I can jog part of the way and if I can change clothes in your room."

"What will you change into?"

"I just happen to have my gym bag in the trunk. I keep it in there just in case I find the time to get a workout in before I go home at night."

Roark in a pair of gym shorts. The image and the feelings it inspired sent a heated blush to her cheeks. "You're on," she said, reminding herself again that he was the enemy. Her only reason for spending time with him was to find her sister.

Still, the thought of being alone with him in her room while the two of them slipped into something far more comfortable and much skimpier touched a few nerves. She would have to be very careful not to mistake the sensual awareness that sizzled between them as a reason to trust him.

If he was able to ignite desire inside her, it was only because he was trained well in the art of seduction—and because it had been a long, long time since she'd been with a man. Actually she'd never been with one who affected her like Roark Lansing. She intended to keep it that way for a while longer.

THE HOTEL ROOM was actually a three-room suite, neat as a pin, no clothes tossed on a chair, no towels on the floor, no empty water glasses or soft-drink cans sitting on the furniture. Roark wasn't surprised. It fit the description Lisa had given of her sister. Always in control, made sound decisions but took few risks, even though she had enough money to afford risks. Worked long hours, took few vacations and never left her bed unmade.

Lisa was in awe of her sister's ability, was certain that she'd never measure up to Kathryn's standards and that Kathryn saw her as a cross she'd been given to bear. Yet all he read from the current situation was that Kathryn was willing to do whatever it took to find Lisa.

He understood the emotion far too well, knew what it was like to search the streets of New Orleans for someone he loved. He still woke up in the middle of the night, bathed in a cold sweat as he relived the pain of finding out that the one he'd been searching for was dead.

"Could I get you something to drink?" Kathryn asked.

"A glass of ice water would be good."

She walked to a mini refrigerator, opened the door

and pulled out two bottles of spring water. "Would you like a glass?"

"I'd feel a lot more at home with the bottle."

She opened them both and handed one to him.

"Nice setup," he said, setting his gym bag on the coffee table. He took a few steps, positioning himself so that he could see the whole suite. "This is almost as big as my apartment and a lot more luxurious. Do you always travel in such style?"

"Not always. This is a business trip and I sometimes need to have people up here for drinks or to discuss projects. I don't want to feel cramped."

"A living area, a dining area and a bedroom with a king-size bed. Don't know how you could feel cramped here. What is there left to miss?"

"My home office, a workout room, my laundry area and my deck and small flower garden."

He gave a low whistle. "You live well. Is there also a husband at this paradise in the suburbs?" He already knew the answer to that question, but he didn't want to give away that he knew not only the general facts of her life, but thanks to Lisa, all sorts of intimate details, as well. Never married. Never even engaged and hadn't dated anyone seriously in months.

"There's no husband, and I don't live in the suburbs. I have a town house near my work. It saves commuting time."

"Commuting where?"

"Excuse me?"

"What town?" He dropped to the sofa and sank into the cushions. "Don't tell me. Let me guess. Definitely in the south. And I hear a drawl. Is it Texan?"

"You're good. It's…Austin."

She'd come close to slipping up, had almost said

Dallas. That worried him. If she wasn't any better at hiding her identity from Devlin, he just might put two and two together and realize who she was and why she was in New Orleans. Roark had always thought Devlin capable of anything to get what he wanted. Now that he'd heard the news about Raycine, he was sure of it. And Devlin wanted Lisa's trust fund.

"You can use the powder room off the living area to change," Kathryn said. "I'll take the bedroom."

"Sounds good."

He watched her walk away, head high as always, back straight, model posture, the black trousers a perfect fit, probably very expensive. He was certain Devlin had noticed all of that, as well. Noticed and been attracted.

Apprehension gnawed at Roark's composure as he picked up his gym bag and stepped into the powder room to change into his running shorts. Kathryn had class, money and intelligence. He had very little of any of those assets, mostly operated on obsession and gut instinct. Kathryn played by the rules. He was willing to break every one in the book. And neither of them seemed a match for Devlin.

Kathryn just wanted to find her sister and know she was safe.

He wanted revenge—at any price. He'd kill Devlin with his bare hands if it came to that. Kill him even if it meant he'd rot in jail for the rest of his life.

A man did what he had to or he ceased to be a man.

THE HUMIDITY was unbelievably high for a day in early December. Perspiration pooled between Kathryn's breasts and rolled down to soak the elastic bottom of her sports bra. They had started down the neutral ground at a fast walk, but when Roark had broken into a jog a couple of blocks later, she'd joined him, matching his pace stride for stride. He'd looked surprised, then smiled broadly when he realized she was no novice to the running scene.

She liked the slight pain that came from pounding the hard ground as she ran, the strain to her muscles, the way her mind seemed to blow out the cobwebs and regain its focus. It was the first time she'd felt halfway normal since she'd gotten the call from the attorney saying he'd heard from someone claiming to be Lisa.

They ran another half mile, still heading away from the hotel. She brushed her wrist band across her forehead. "Don't you think we should turn around?"

"Are you getting tired?" His voice was punctuated by short, choppy breaths.

"It's the humidity. I'm not used to it."

"You mean if it was cool and dry, you'd really kick my butt?"

"I might." And a nice butt it was. Firm. Tight. She dropped behind for a closer look. His thighs were pretty spectacular, as well. There were men in Dallas who looked just as good in a pair of running shorts. She noticed them, but they never affected her the way Roark did.

He slowed and positioned himself at her side. "We're only a couple of blocks from Audubon Park. Can you make it that far?"

"Can I collapse when I get there?"

"Under giant oak trees."

"Then I'll make it."

"We can slow to a walk if you need to."

"And let an old man like you get the better of me?"

"Hey, who's old? I have two more weeks before I hit thirty-nine."

"Then you should be able to keep up." Eleven years older than her. She'd have guessed more like five. She tapped him on the arm with her fist, then sprinted ahead. She was breathing hard by the time they reached the park, her lungs burning. There was a fortunate lull in traffic and she slowed to a walk as she crossed the street and took a cement path that meandered off the sidewalk. When she reached the first tree, she fell to the carpet of grass, taking full advantage of the shade provided by the sparse brown leaves still clinging to the branches.

A young mother walked by, pushing a baby in an old-fashioned carriage. Two teenagers flew by on their in-line skates, and a young man a few yards away was strumming a guitar. Roark was nowhere in sight.

Foreboding stole the placid feel of the moment. He'd been right behind her. Surely he'd seen her take the path into the park. This was ridiculous. He was a grown man on a busy street. It was the events of the past few days that had her paranoid and so quick to jump to fear.

Still, she didn't relax until he jogged into view. He spotted her at once, and a few seconds later he dropped to the ground beside her, two large oranges and a couple of bottles of water in hand. "I thought we might need these."

"Where did you get them?"

"Some guy was standing out there selling fruit to people who stopped at the traffic light."

"Fruit and water?"

"No, the water was for him. I talked him out of them—for twice their original price, of course."

"And worth every penny." She unscrewed the top and took a large gulp. "I can't remember when water tasted so good."

"You would if you'd jogged in New Orleans this past summer. Nothing like the Big Easy for heat and humidity." He tossed her an orange.

She peeled it and slid one of the wedges into her mouth. The juice squirted out, some spilling onto her lips. She licked them clean.

"How is it?"

"Sweet and juicy. Thanks." She peeled off another wedge of the fruit and fed it to him. Her fingers brushed his lips and a rush of heat shot through her. Damn. Every time she touched him, it was as if a jagged streak of lightning flashed between them.

She pulled her hand away and stared at the ground, determined to pull herself together. It was harder this time, more difficult to convince herself that Roark was the enemy, that he was part of Mystic Isle and she had no reason to trust him.

Roark stretched out on the grass, pulled his baseball cap down so that it sheltered his face from the sun that filtered through the tree branches. She could see the corners of his eyes, knew they were shut tight, and he lay so still she thought he might have gone to sleep. She stretched out beside him, on her side so that she could see the steady rise and fall of his chest as his breathing settled down to a normal rate.

The need to touch him was almost overpowering. Or maybe it was just the need to touch anyone, to reach out and have someone be there. To have one afternoon when she didn't feel as if the weight of the world rested on her shoulders. To have one day when she simply took life and didn't feel the need to control it.

Lisa did that all the time, frequently reached out to the wrong people, but at least she reached out. Kathryn had resented her ability to do that, always thought it was immature and irresponsible of her to meet someone and connect instantly on so many different levels.

And yet here she was doing the same thing with Roark Lansing. Needing desperately to trust him when she knew she couldn't. She was in this by herself. Kathryn, the rescuer. Only, when would anybody ever rescue her? When would someone even realize she needed rescuing from her inability to rely on someone besides herself?

The answer was probably never.

Roark stretched his arms over his head, his body growing tight and then relaxing, his T-shirt riding up so that a band of bare flesh showed between his shorts and shirt. Bronze skin peppered with a few dark hairs. The need inside her became an ache. She touched her hand to the flat of his stomach.

Without opening his eyes, he reached out, pulled her into his arms and kissed her.

Chapter Seven

Roark drowned in the kiss, in the thrill of the moment, in the salty taste of Kathryn's lips. He hadn't planned to let this happen, not even when he'd seen her walk out of her bedroom in her form-fitting running shorts and the cropped white T-shirt. Not even when he'd run behind her and watched the movement of her tight little behind.

He hadn't planned for it to happen, but now that it had, he couldn't get enough. His hands tangled in her hair, and he kissed her again and again, hungry, wet kisses that fed his soul. For a second, he closed the world out, the scams, the deceit, the murders. Then it all came back in a body-numbing rush.

He kissed her once more, then pulled away, slowly, almost painfully. When he met her gaze, he realized that whatever insane emotion had taken over his mind and body had evidently taken over hers, as well. The cool and unflappable Kathryn Morland was flushed.

She sat up, but didn't move away from him. "Wow! You New Orleans guys do know how to end a run."

She was obviously aiming for nonchalance, but the breathless catch in her voice gave her away. Roark propped himself up on his elbows. "We like to keep the tourists happy."

She looked away and stared at a blade of grass she'd pulled from one of her socks. "They should print that in the tour guide. Or maybe Devlin should include it in his flyers. It gives a whole new meaning to the term 'harmony of the spirits.'"

Her tone had taken on a jagged edge. Apparently she'd moved past the magic of the moment and back into reality. "The kiss had nothing to do with Devlin or Mystic Isle, Kathryn."

"Then why did you kiss me?"

"For the same reason you kissed me back. I'm a man. You're a woman. We're attracted to each other and we kissed. I don't know that there was any reasoning involved."

There certainly hadn't been on his part. If he'd thought beyond the moment, he'd never have kissed her, never have let himself become vulnerable. His emotions were already bruised and raw, the heartbreak of nine months ago ripped open and laid bare with the knowledge that another young woman had been murdered. This time right under his nose.

"I'm sorry, Roark. I overreacted. You're right. It was just a kiss. It didn't mean anything."

That wasn't what he'd said and certainly not the truth. The kiss had meant a lot of things—none of them right. He had to keep focused, and the last thing he needed was to care about anyone, especially Kathryn Morland. What he really needed was for her to catch the next flight back to Dallas, but he'd given up on that. The next best thing was to keep her away from Devlin. That wasn't likely to happen, either. He was losing all the way around.

"I guess it's time we went back."

Kathryn stretched her legs in front of her and groaned. "I'm not sure I can make it."

"Going back is easy. I'll hail a cab." He stood and tugged her to her feet, and they started walking down the pathway to the Avenue. The kiss had been a mistake, but the running had been a good idea. He'd have to keep his emotions in check, but he did need to spend time with Kathryn if only to keep her safe.

And he had to make sure that Devlin didn't find out that she was Lisa's sister and was there to rescue Lisa and her money from his clutches. He had his work cut out for him. Roark Lansing, man of mystery, keeper of the keys to the shop at Mystic Isle, the right-hand man to the powerful and charismatic Devlin Tishe.

But it was the keys to Tujacque's Manor he needed. Access to secret files. Evidence of murder. His cell phone shrilled. He pulled it from his waist and punched the talk number. "Hello."

"Roark. It's Lisa."

The irony of the situation hit hard. Kathryn by his side. Lisa on the phone and sounding extremely upset. "What's up?"

"I'm scared, really scared."

"Not another snake on the loose?"

"I wish it was. It's Raycine, Roark. She's been murdered."

Kathryn appeared to be taking in the scenery, but he knew she was listening to the conversation. He had to watch every word. "Did someone tell you that?"

"Of course not. No one tells me anything now that I'm stuck in this hellhole. I overheard Cottonmouth talking on the phone. Raycine's body was pulled out of Bayou St. John. Foul play suspected. That means murder, doesn't it?''

"Most likely."

"And I had to learn about it by accident. I was outside Cottonmouth's door about to knock when I heard him mention my name and say he wouldn't tell me a thing. I stayed there and listened to the rest of the conversation."

"Do you know who he was talking to?"

"He didn't say a name, but I'm sure it was Veretha. He was using that voice he always uses with her, like she's some kind of queen and he's the dutiful servant. I hate that woman, I really do."

"Okay. You need to settle down a little."

"Settle down! Are you crazy? Veretha hated Raycine because Devlin needed her. She hates me even more. She killed Raycine, and she'll kill me next. I have to talk to Devlin, Roark. You have to find him for me. I have to tell him everything. Veretha's crazy. She may kill him, too."

Her words tumbled over each other, running on and on. Roark let her talk without interrupting.

"I've been in my room. With my door locked. I've been trying to call Devlin for the last half hour, but he doesn't answer. Please, Roark. Find him for me. I have to talk to him."

"I'll take care of it, but I want you to listen carefully. Turn your phone off and leave it off until I get there. No phone calls to or from anyone."

"Not even Devlin?"

"*No one.* I'll explain when I get there, but it's important."

"Then you'll have to come now, Roark. I'm going crazy."

"I'll be there in an hour. Stay in your room and wait for me."

"If you say so."

"I do."

"I want to get out of this place—tonight."

"We'll talk when I get there."

His hand was shaking as he broke the connection.

Kathryn lay a hand on his arm. "You look upset. Is something wrong?"

"A friend of mine just got some bad news."

A friend. Kathryn's sister, finally realizing she was playing games with her life. He felt like a heel for not telling Kathryn what was going on, but dragging her into the deadly mix would make him far worse than a heel.

Fortunately they didn't have to wait long for a taxi. Roark tried to make small talk on the ride back to the hotel but failed miserably. After a few attempts, he quit trying. The game was heating to a fevered pitch. The stakes were twelve million dollars, sweet revenge, and life and death.

They rode the last few blocks in silence while he concentrated on what he had to do and how he had to do it in order to get what he wanted and still keep Lisa and Kathryn alive.

DEVLIN STOOD in his office on the second floor of the Esplanade Avenue mansion and stared at the sleek leather-and-chrome furnishings, the trappings of success. Not that any of it was actually his. The house and furnishings were mortgaged to the hilt, and he never paid more than the minimum amount required on any account. That way he had less to lose when he walked away.

He'd been in New Orleans five years, three of them in this place that Veretha had dubbed Mystic Isle, the longest period of time he'd ever been in one place. In some ways he'd miss it when he left. In another way he would be glad to be rid of the cumbersome burden of pretending to believe in the ridiculous doctrine he'd dreamed up one night after he and Veretha had drunk way too much tequila.

He remembered the night well. They had been out in the Gulf of Mexico, just off the coast of Louisiana, on an overnight excursion to the real Mystic Isle. A desolate barrier island, swept clean by relentless winds and the constant spray of waves.

Most of the year the island was deserted except for visits by the occasional fisherman, but once a year, at the winter solstice, it was visited by a strange band of men and women, all intent on fulfilling earthly desires while worshiping hellish spirits. On that one night, the island came alive to bizarre chants and sacrificial rituals so heathen and barbaric that even Devlin had found them frightening.

He'd done it then for Veretha. At that point he'd been so totally infatuated with her he would have done anything to be with her. Somewhere along the way, the infatuation had dissolved into mild lust. Their lovemaking had lost the exotic flames that had fueled it in the beginning. Another sign it was time to move on.

He would turn his back and walk away from the life he was living and everything in it, the way he'd done so many times before. But this time there was one very big difference. This time he'd be leaving town a multimillionaire. All he needed was Lisa Morland's trust fund safely deposited in one of his bank accounts in the Cayman Islands. And that was practically a done deal. The beautiful and sensual Lizemera was putty in his hands.

Staying out of jail until the money was assured was his only problem. Once Raycine's father realized she'd had anything to do with Mystic Isle, Devlin would be the prime suspect. Policemen never trusted men like him, anyway.

He went to the closet and pulled one of his silvery gray robes from the hanger. Mrs. Samuel Orton III was waiting in the Awakening Room, expecting to commune with her departed husband. He'd make certain she wasn't disappointed. Five thousand dollars was a pittance compared to Lisa's twelve million, but he needed to conduct business as usual until he was ready to charter a jet to Mexico.

Do nothing to alert anyone of your next move. He'd never seen the rule printed anywhere, but it was one every good con man adhered to. And he was one of the best.

IT WAS DARK by the time Roark drove into the curved drive and stopped in front of Tujacque's Manor. The temperature had dropped into the high fifties at sundown, but the wind whipping through the trees made it feel much colder. He grabbed his windbreaker from the back seat of the car, along with the big brown envelope stuffed with blank sheets of paper and the Burger King bag. By the time he reached the steps, Cottonmouth was waiting for him at the door.

"Hey, buddy," Roark said, plastering a smile on his face. "How's it going?"

"Going all right." Cottonmouth stared at the Burger King bag. "Whatcha got there?"

"A couple of Whoppers with cheese, a large order of fries and a chocolate shake."

"Who you brung them for?"

"You, if you want them."

"Don't never turn down a cheeseburger." He took the bag in his meaty hand. "Nobody told me you was comin' out here tonight. Veretha send you to check on Lisa?"

"Nope. Not to check on her." Roark patted the brown envelope he'd tucked under his left arm. "I brought her some work. Is she around?"

"I reckon she is. Ain't nowhere to go without a car, not when you're stuck this far out in the boondocks." Cottonmouth moved aside so that Roark could come into the wide foyer. "She's been in her room by herself all afternoon. Probably in one of her pouting moods."

Roark stepped close and kept his voice low. "She's doesn't know about Raycine, does she?"

"If she does, she ain't said nothin' about it. And she sure didn't hear it from me. Want me to get her for you?"

"No, that's okay. I'll go up there. I need the exercise."

"Suit yourself." Cottonmouth already had one of his big hands buried in the Burger King bag. "I'll be back in my room watching my TV shows."

Roark climbed the two flights of stairs. Damn. He needed more time. Just a few more days and his mission would have been accomplished. Finally he'd have had a shred of closure, and Devlin would have gotten what he deserved.

Mariah Carey's voice wafted from beneath Lisa's door, one of the same CDs she listened to over and over. He knocked and waited. He could hear her footsteps as she crossed the room.

"Who's there?" He could tell from her voice she'd been crying.

"Roark."

She opened the door and threw herself into his arms like a kid who'd just been rescued from a fierce dog. He pushed her back inside, never certain if Cottonmouth was watching from around the corner or if there were cameras hidden in the shadows. And Tujacque's Manor had more than its share of cobweb-filled corners and shadows.

"I was afraid you wouldn't come," she said, backing away.

"I told you I would."

"I know, but it's hard to know who I can trust these days."

"I understand." And he did, all too well.

"I definitely don't trust Veretha. Neither does Devlin." She stepped back, dropped into a worn upholstered chair in the corner and curled her feet beneath the folds of her long full skirt.

Her pale-blond hair draped across her shoulders, her bangs falling over her eyebrows and framing her red swollen eyes. She looked much younger than she was. Thinner than she'd been a month ago, pale in the flickering light from a half-dozen candles scattered about the room, as fragile as the spirits Devlin produced at will back at Mystic Isle.

He looked at her and felt new pangs of the sickening dread that had all but broken his heart in the first days after he'd gotten the news that Margie was dead. Had she ended up like this? Alone? Shivering in the dark? Waiting to be killed?

Lisa clutched a shredded tissue in her hands. "Poor Raycine. I keep thinking it's all a mistake and she'll open the door and walk in here any second. I just can't believe she's really dead."

He pulled up a chair and sat right in front of her, close enough they could have touched. "She's dead, Lisa."

"I'm not Lisa. I'm Lizemera, the chosen one. Only I don't want to be Lizemera or one of the chosen. Raycine was chosen and look what happened to her." She wiped the back of her hand across her cheek and caught an escaping tear. "I don't feel any harmony or peace anymore, Roark. All I feel is grief—and fear. I wish Devlin was here. He'd know how to make me feel better. He always does."

Roark took her hands in his. "Even Devlin can't bring Raycine back. No one can do that."

"I know. But he could take me away from here."

"Where would you go?"

"Home. Back to Dallas. I can wait for Devlin there. When Veretha goes to jail, he'll come to me."

There was no way in heaven or hell Devlin was going to let Lisa just walk away before he got his hands on her money, and no way Roark would be able to convince her of that. As for Veretha and Cottonmouth, he had no idea what they were capable of, but he knew their loyalties lay with Devlin.

"Talking to Devlin about this could be a big mistake, Lisa. Veretha's his wife. Even if she did have something to do with Raycine's death, I don't think he'd believe you."

When she looked up and met his gaze, her eyes were shadowed with fear.

"You can't say anything to Devlin about this, Lisa.

You can't admit that you know about Raycine's murder.''

"I can't keep this up forever.''

"You won't have to keep it up forever. Just let it ride for a few more days. If it's not settled by then, I'll come and get you and take you back to Dallas myself.''

"I can't lie to Devlin.''

"Then don't lie to him. Don't say anything at all.''

His insides churned. If he left now without telling Lisa more, he knew she'd go to Devlin. She was wrong about a lot of things, but she was right about one. She was likely the next victim on the hit list. If she kept quiet, she'd be safe until her birthday. Devlin needed her alive in order to get his hands on her money. Roark had learned that much through his own snooping.

But if she started talking, if Devlin was forced to run before he was ready, she'd be dead. He had no choice but to tell her at least part of the truth.

"I want you to listen to me very carefully, Lisa. Raycine was killed by someone connected with Mystic Isle, but not for the reason you think.''

"Then what reason?''

"I know this is going to sound bizarre to you, but she accidentally ran across some secret files while she was working on the investigations she was doing for Devlin.''

"But the investigations were just routine. Devlin did them to keep out tabloid reporters and others who wanted to spread lies and damage his ministry.''

It constantly amazed Roark that reasonably smart women could be so taken in by Devlin. Raycine had even believed that was the purpose of the investigations at first. Then gradually she'd realized that Devlin was running a scam operation, that the investigations were merely to find out who the good risks were and what they were worth.

That was when Raycine had switched sides, started investigating Devlin and his operations in secret. But Lisa was nowhere near accepting the truth about Devlin. Roark would have to walk a very tight line with her, not do anything to send her running to the *master*. "Nonetheless," he continued, "Raycine ran across something that concerned her."

"Did she go to Devlin and ask him about it?"

"No. She came to me. The information had to do with some practices that she thought were illegal, and she thought Devlin might be in on them."

Lisa shook her head. "She never said anything to me."

"That's because she knows how much you love Devlin. She didn't want to upset you." And she knew damn well Lisa wouldn't believe her, just as he knew he couldn't hit her with the full truth even now.

"What kind of illegal practices?"

"I'm not certain."

"Then why didn't she just go to the police? Her father's a cop. He would have helped her."

"She thought she could find out more than anyone else. She had access to the computer here at Tujacque's Manor, and she was an expert at hacking, at finding secret passwords and unlocking files. I think she found what she was looking for, Lisa. And that's why someone killed her."

Lisa jumped up from the chair and paced the room. "Veretha killed her, Roark. We have to tell Devlin. If we don't, she may kill him, too."

He stood and caught her in his arms as she passed. He had to make her listen and understand. "Veretha won't kill Devlin, Lisa. But she might kill you if she thinks you know something. You have to convince her *and* Devlin that you don't.''

Lisa pulled away from him and walked to the window to stare out into the dark of a moonless night. ''Veretha is behind everything, Roark. She's evil, a reincarnated viper. That's why she can handle those snakes without getting bitten. She's one of them.''

''If that's the case, I should have proof in a few days. When we have the evidence, we can go to Devlin and to the police.''

''So that's why you've been out here so often lately and why you've been so eager to help me run the investigations of new people who attend Devlin's lectures.''

''That's the main reason.''

''I want to help you, Roark. I can get on the computer any time I want to. All you have to do is tell me what to look for.''

His insides quaked. This was exactly what he needed and yet he couldn't put Lisa in harm's way. ''No. It's too dangerous. I can't take chances with your life.''

''You won't be taking chances. I will.''

''I can't let you do it.''

''Please, Roark,'' she begged. ''I have to do something to help or I'll go crazy. Raycine was my friend. Don't you understand what that means? I'll stay here and keep quiet just like you asked, but only if you'll tell me how to search for the files.''

''You aren't giving me much choice.''

''More than Veretha gave Raycine.''

Roark dropped back onto the chair. ''Then sit down and listen. I can tell you how to reach a certain point. After that, it's trial and error. You have to keep all of this in your head. If you write anything down, there's a chance someone will see your notes and know what you're doing.''

''Okay. I have just one other request.''

''What's that?''

''I tried to call my sister today, but the cellular phone service says my call-out numbers have been restricted. I want you to call her and tell her that I'm safe. Don't tell her where I am or what I'm doing. Just tell her that I'm okay and that I'll see her soon.''

''I'll tell her.''

But how would he ever tell her if he let harm come to Lisa?

He was still thinking about Kathryn a half hour later when he left the plantation house and started down the deserted road that led back to civilization. If there was anyone truly innocent in this whole thing, it was Kathryn.

Yet she was jumping headfirst into the most deadly waters of all. Going after Devlin Tishe all by herself. Headstrong, foolishly brave, determined. Maybe that was why he couldn't get her off his mind. When he could stand it no longer, he picked up the phone and punched in the number for the Pontchartrain Hotel.

Chapter Eight

The phone rang about six times before a hotel operator picked up and informed Roark that the guest he was calling was apparently out. When asked if he'd like to leave a message, he declined. Even if she'd answered, the call would have been a mistake.

He had no intention of giving her Lisa's message. If he did, she'd squash any chance he had of getting the evidence to put Devlin away and she'd put both herself and Lisa in more danger than they were already in. She'd be furious if she learned he knew where Lisa was and that she was safe and hadn't told her. She'd break off all contact with him and he couldn't protect her. And anything else he said would sound as if he was desperate to see her again, or just plain harassing her.

The truth of why he'd called probably lay somewhere in the middle. He did feel a near-compelling need to hear her voice. But mainly he needed to reassure himself that she was safely in her room, still content to give herself time to get to know him and Devlin before she jumped into the fray with both feet kicking and fists flying.

Unfortunately he didn't get that reassurance.

He flicked on the radio and got the top-of-the-hour news. The talk was all about the lifeless body of Raycine Ranklin being pulled from the bayou that ran right through one of the prettiest parts of town. The full autopsy report was not being released, but the preliminary indication was that she'd been strangled, dead before she'd been buried in her watery grave.

Murders were commonplace. The fact that Raycine was the daughter of a New Orleans homicide detective gave this one clout. It also meant that the local authorities would go after the killer with a vengeance.

And sooner or later, someone would mention that Raycine had attended lectures at Mystic Isle and become fascinated with the theory of harmony between the spirits of good and evil. And when they did, the cops would come calling at Mystic Isle—all because of a very stupid mistake that didn't sound at all like the work of the infamous Devlin Tishe.

There were dozens of ways to dispose of a body so that it wouldn't be found anytime soon. Dumping it into the shallow bayou wasn't one of them. So, assuming Devlin had either killed Raycine or had her killed, why hadn't he had her buried in some godforsaken plot of earth near Tujacque's Manor? Or dropped her where she'd have been lunch for a hungry gator? Or, better yet, had her cremated and stored her ashes in some Egyptian urn in one of the eerie, seemingly haunted rooms on the second floor of Mystic Isle.

Damn. He hated that these kinds of thoughts were even stalking his mind. Gory and morbid, and so much a part of what he'd become over the past nine months. Still, it seemed incredibly stupid to dispose of a young woman and let her body be found within days of the time Devlin planned to get his hands on Lisa Morland's trust fund.

Unless Devlin wasn't behind the murder at all.

No. Devlin was the leader. Nothing came down without his say-so—except Veretha's bizarre fascination with reclaiming her position as a voodoo priestess and with practicing ancient rituals. And that had nothing to do with Raycine.

Devlin had killed Raycine and he'd killed Margie, likely for the same reasons. Sooner or later, smart women caught on to him. There was no telling how many others had been killed for similar reasons.

It was way past time Devlin paid for his crimes. But even Roark now had to admit that it might never happen.

KATHRYN WALKED down the middle of Bourbon Street, thoughts of the nightly news running through her mind. Raycine Ranklin, daughter of NOPD Detective Butch Ranklin, had been found dead in a New Orleans bayou near City Park. Only two days ago he had been telling her she shouldn't worry about her missing sister. She doubted he'd tell her the same thing now.

Her heart went out to the detective and his wife. Their only daughter lost to them forever because someone in this town had strangled her and dumped her body into a bayou. Kathryn ached for the Ranklins and for herself. But mostly she just worried about where Lisa was tonight and if she was safe.

Her walk slowed to a crawl, though she'd been here before, seen the rows of small shops selling T-shirts, masks, boxes of pralines and all the usual tourist temptations. Watched the mimes, their bodies covered in paint, standing on the street corners, motionless, waiting for the meager tips to be dropped into the boxes at their feet.

She listened to the lone musician playing jazz on a saxophone and the music that spilled from the open doorways of small clubs crowded between the strip clubs and souvenir shops. Smelled the mouthwatering aroma from the hot dog vendors and the almost over-powering odor of beer that flowed from the countless bars and onto the street via large plastic cups.

The sights, the sounds, the smells all registered in Kathryn's mind, but it was as if they were being filtered through massive layers of gauze. All she really saw were the people, especially young women near Lisa's age. She stared into their faces, looked into their eyes, hoped that some strange quirk of fate would bring her face-to-face with her sister. Lisa was a natural blonde, but that meant nothing. Her sister changed her hair color on a whim, the same way she changed her friends or her interests. Perhaps the same way she'd changed her address.

She could be anywhere, yet Kathryn was convinced that not only was she in New Orleans, she was still connected to Devlin Tishe in some way. A lover? Hidden away and waiting to receive her inheritance so that they could ride away into the sunset together?

Or had she become disillusioned and bored with Devlin the way she tired of everything and everyone after a season and just walked away? Was she on the streets tonight, hanging out with the wrong crowd? Or had she ceased to exist at all, the same way Detective Ranklin's daughter had ceased to exist?

Dread settled over Kathryn like a stifling black shroud, and she swallowed hard, determined not to become sick. She picked up her pace, her heart pounding as she walked block after block. By the time she collected her wits, she realized she'd left the crowds. The street was dark, the storefronts mostly unlit. A drunk sprawled in a doorway, and the nauseating odor of whiskey and unwashed body assailed her as she stepped around him. Two young men walked together on the other side of the street and an older man leaned against a car about half a block away.

She'd wandered too far from the Quarter, ventured into areas where tourists were warned not to go by themselves. Turning on her heel, she started back in the direction she'd come. It had been a mistake to come here tonight. She couldn't just walk through the crowded streets of a major city and expect Lisa to materialize before her eyes. Things like that only happened in movies.

"Hey, lady. You got some money you can give me? I haven't eaten today."

She turned at the youthful voice. A girl who couldn't have been a day over fifteen had appeared as if from nowhere. Homeless, begging on the street. She probably walked all over this part of town, knew where people... Suddenly a new possibility popped into Kathryn's mind.

"I don't have any money to give," she answered, looking at the girl and wondering if she could trust her, or if a half-dozen just like her were waiting in the shadows for her to open her purse. "If you're really hungry, I could hire you, though."

The girl stared at her, then shook her head. "I don't do no funny stuff."

"No, I'd just like you to look at a picture and see if you recognize the young woman I'm looking for."

"You want me to squeal on someone." The girl

pushed back a mop of spiky bright-red hair. "You a stinkin' cop?" She added a few four-letter words, probably hoping to sound tough.

"No, I'm just looking for my sister. I need to talk to her."

"How much you gonna pay me?"

"Twenty dollars for looking at the picture. A hundred if you take me to her."

"A hundred dollars. You serious?"

"If you take me to her."

"Let's see the picture."

Kathryn looked around. The man who'd been leaning on the car half a block away had moved a lot closer, was standing in the shadows puffing on a cigarette not more than thirty feet from where she and the girl stood. She was more certain than ever that this was no place to unzip her fanny pack and pull out her wallet. "Walk over to Jackson Square with me. I'll buy you a sandwich and some soup at Le Madeleine and show you the picture there."

"You'll buy the food and still give me the whole twenty?"

"That's the deal."

The girl looked around and nodded, a signal to someone. Just as Kathryn had suspected, she hadn't been alone. Then Kathryn and the girl started back toward Canal Street, walking side by side like old friends. No funny stuff, the girl had said, yet she was living on the streets, begging for food. Kathryn couldn't help but wonder if there was a mother somewhere in a loving home who lay awake nights worrying about this girl the way she worried about Lisa.

Or was the life the girl had run away from a hundred times worse than the new one she'd found? There were homes like that, where a girl of fifteen had to live in hell or run.

But Lisa wasn't fifteen, and she hadn't run *away* from anything. She'd just run to something new, the way she always did. Experimenting. Jumping in without a second thought, trusting that Kathryn, the enabler, would come to her rescue. Only this time she might have jumped in too deep for Kathryn to save her.

IT WAS TEN before ten when Kathryn and the girl, who only gave her name as Punch, slid into two wooden chairs at a small round table by the window. Kathryn had eaten a chef salad at the hotel earlier, but she ordered a bowl of tomato-basil soup. Her guest took full advantage of the free meal. She'd ordered half a rotisserie-roasted chicken with potatoes and a salad and an apricot-filled Danish pastry that looked big enough for a family of four. They both chose the French roast coffee, but Punch weakened hers with an ample helping of steamed milk.

The girl ate as if afraid someone would come to the table and snatch the food away at any second, tearing off the chicken with her fingers and shoveling it into her mouth. Kathryn was so totally intrigued with watching that she let her own soup grow lukewarm before she took the first bite.

Punch's plate was more than half-empty before she seemed to even remember that Kathryn was there. "So this woman you're looking for," Punch said, stopping to lick her fingers, "is she a druggie or a prostitute— or both?"

"Neither."

"Yeah, well, this ain't no Sunday school down here,

you know, not for those living on the streets, anyway. So what does she do?''

''I'm not sure. All I know is that she moved to the city and that she had an apartment a few blocks from here for a while.''

''If you have an apartment, you gotta get money somewhere. What kind of work did she do?''

''I don't think she had a job.''

''Probably turning tricks, then. She in trouble?''

''I hope not. I'd just like to find her.''

''Are you sure you're her sister and not her parole officer?''

''I'm her sister. All I'd like for you to do is look at the picture and tell me if you've seen her, and if so, where.''

''That's for the twenty. And if I take you to her, you come up with a croaker?''

''Excuse me?''

''A croaker. You know. A buck. A hundred-dollar bill.''

''Right.'' Kathryn unzipped her fanny pack and pulled out a wallet-size snapshot of Lisa. She passed it across the table. Thankfully Punch wiped her greasy hands on her napkin before she took it from Kathryn's hand.

She stared at the photo and her lips drew into a tight strained line.

''Her name's Lisa Morland,'' Kathryn said. ''What do you know about her?''

''Nothing.'' Punch shook her head and handed the snapshot back to Kathryn. ''I've never seen her.''

Kathryn's hand shook as she set her half-empty coffee cup down on the table. ''Don't give me that. I saw the look on your face when you looked at the picture. You've seen her and you know something about her.''

Punch shook her head vehemently. ''You know what? I don't see any family resemblance in that picture. I don't think you're her sister at all.''

''Then who do you think I am?''

''I don't know. I don't give a damn.'' Punch spread her napkin on the table. The chair skidded behind her as she stood. ''You owe me twenty bucks.''

Kathryn removed two twenties from her wallet. She started to pull out one of her business cards, as well, then thought better of it. Instead, she scribbled her cell-phone number down on a clean napkin and handed it to Punch, along with the money. ''As I said, my sister's name is Lisa Morland. If you change your mind and decide to talk, call me at this number. And I'm raising the ante. Five hundred dollars if you tell me where she is.''

Punch took the napkin, studied it for a few seconds, then stuffed it into her jeans pocket. ''Exactly what do I have to do for the five hundred?''

''Tell me where she is. If she's there, you get the money.''

''And you'll keep my name out of everything?''

''If that's the way you want it. So, do you know where she is?''

''No, but I can give you the name of someone who might. What's that worth to you?''

''Just a name of a person who might or might not help me? Not worth much.''

''It's more than you have now.''

''You're right. Fifty dollars.'' Kathryn unzipped her fanny pack, this time removing two twenties and a ten.

She laid them on the table, but kept her hand planted on top of them. "What's the name?"

Punch mouthed the name, rather than saying it out loud, but Kathryn had no difficulty reading her lips. The name was Veretha Tishe. She lifted her hand from the bills and Punch grabbed them fast and disappeared out a side door.

Veretha Tishe. Back to square one. Only how had Punch known that and why had seeing Lisa's picture upset her?

Kathryn finished her coffee before walking to Chartres St. to catch a cab back to the hotel. Now she had three leads, all connected to Mystic Isle.

Veretha was a petite woman who moved with the agility of a cat and the sexuality of an exotic princess. Devlin was bigger than life, a man who preached a doctrine of peace and harmony with the fervor of an evangelist. Roark was mysterious, sexy, almost bewitching. When she was with him, she lost her edge, let down her guard, reeled from a devastating attraction that had no practical basis.

All roads still led to Mystic Isle. So far they'd all been dead ends. But she wasn't about to give up yet.

VERETHA CLIMBED from the king-size bed she still shared with her husband, though the past few months they seldom did more than sleep together or practice boring sex. She padded silently across the thick carpet, making her way to the door in the darkness.

There was a time when he hadn't been able to keep his eyes or his hands off her. She'd used all her tricks on him, the things she'd learned on the streets in the ghetto long before she'd changed her name and declared herself a voodoo priestess. Devlin had taught her things, too. They'd been dynamite, wild, devouring every type of sensual pleasure as if every night were the last night of the world.

Now when they made love it was routine, more ritual than riotous, the act without the emotion. He'd told her when they first met that his whole life was a crapshoot. As long as he was winning, he stayed in the game. When the odds changed, he was gone before the next throw of the dice.

The appearance of Raycine's body had just changed the odds. But she knew Devlin well enough to know that he wouldn't drop out of the shoot with almost twelve million dollars riding on the next toss—not unless he was running for his life. Of course, his other option was to run *with* Lisa.

But as far as she was concerned, Lisa and her money were dispensable. After all, she'd never needed wealth to be happy.

And what possible difference would one more body make?

December 5

KATHRYN STRUGGLED with the zipper on her simple black dress, finally working it loose from the pinch of fabric it had bitten into and easing it to the top. Cut low in back, showing just a sliver of cleavage in front, it gave her the image she was after.

Sexy enough to capture Devlin's attention the way she was sure Lisa had. She could never pull off the big-eyed innocence that Lisa did so naturally, but she could feign fascination with what Devlin said, and that had been a big enough turn-on to warrant an invitation to a party at the Tujacque home.

Now she had to make the most of it.

A hard knock sounded at her door. She took a quick glance in the mirror and straightened her hair, pulling it down with her fingers so that her bangs grazed her right eyebrow, then moistened her lips with her tongue.

Ready or not, she was about to go to work on the infamous Devlin Tishe. But when she opened the door, it was Roark Lansing staring back at her. In a black tux and holding a crystal flute of sparkling champagne in each hand. Looking like something straight out of an erotic dream.

"Room Service."

"I didn't order champagne."

"Who's talking about champagne!"

He stepped inside, and her willpower plummeted right through the floor of the historic Pontchartrain Hotel.

Chapter Nine

Roark used his foot to close the door behind him. He stared at Kathryn, aware as always of the tension that crackled between them. It was built on a lot of things. Danger. Lies. Deadly stakes.

And an attraction that knocked him back on his heels. Sexual attraction was like that, came on without warning and stole a man's power to reason with any kind of clarity. Yet, as cynical as he was about anything that even hinted of romance, much less that love-at-first-sight nonsense spread by novels and movies, he knew that what he felt for Kathryn went deeper than just some kind of sensual bombardment.

The attraction was based on a lot more than her looks. It had to do with her commitment to find her sister, the way she'd come to New Orleans and taken on the job herself, even though she had more money in her bank account than he'd make in a lifetime.

And beyond that, he'd liked the way she looked in his pirogue, dressed in faded jeans and a sweatshirt, not bothering with makeup or worrying about the wind blowing her hair. And then there was the way she kissed.

And he damned well better get all of that mushy

bunk out of his mind and get down to business before he made some stupid, machismo-driven mistake. He handed her one of the glasses of champagne. "To get you in a party mood."

She took it without meeting his gaze. "Thank you."

"You're welcome, but it's actually compliments of Devlin Tishe and the limo company."

"A limousine? I had no idea we were traveling in such style. I wouldn't have thought that of a man like Devlin. He seems so detached from the material world."

"Peace and harmony do not prohibit the enjoyment of luxuries."

"True. I guess there's nothing wrong with going first-class."

He let his gaze move to the impressive diamond pendant that graced her long, elegant neck. "I'd say you, too, have a taste for the finer things in life."

"Does that mean you approve of my necklace?"

He stepped closer and touched his fingers to the sparkling gem. The stone was faceted and cold. The skin beneath it was silky smooth and warm. A wave of desire shot through him and he let the jewel slip between his fingers. "It's as lovely as the woman wearing it."

"Thanks. It belonged to my mother, a gift from her mother on her wedding day. I never wear it without thinking of both of them." She held up her glass of champagne. "We should toast."

"Your call," he said. "What will it be?"

"To an informative evening with new friends."

"Just informative? Not enjoyable or entertaining?"

"To all of that and more."

"I'll drink to that."

They clinked their glasses together, like old friends,

instead of conspirators bound by mistrust on her part
and wariness on his.

She sipped her champagne. "Will we be picking up
Devlin and Veretha?"

"They're already in the car. Grace Tujacque's home
is only a mile or so from here, right down the Avenue."

"Then we shouldn't keep them waiting. We can fin-
ish our drinks on the way." She took one last look in
the mirror, then reached for a red velvet cape thrown
across the back of a chair.

He took it from her hands and spread it over her
shoulders. His thumbs touched, then lingered on her
neck just below her earlobes, as the fragrance of her
perfume rocked his resolve. Five more minutes alone
with her and he'd be in big trouble. Five more seconds
of touching her might do it.

He stepped away and opened the door. "Your carriage awaits." He motioned for her to precede him.

She touched his arm. "Wait, Roark."

His breath caught. Her tone had grown too serious.
He didn't want her to confess anything to him, didn't
want her to trust him when he couldn't give her what
she wanted. And even if she trusted him now, she'd
hate him when she discovered he'd been lying to her
all along. His muscles clenched. His insides churned.
"Is there a problem, Kathryn?"

"I need to—" She stopped midsentence, but he
could read the doubt in her eyes. Then she shook her
head and walked toward him. "No problem. No problem at all."

They both knew she was lying.

THE GRANDEUR of the Tujacque home struck Kathryn
from the second the limo pulled into the curved drive

of the pillared mansion. The veranda was wide, the sheltering trees majestic, the house rambling out in all directions, stacked three floors high and topped with turrets. The effect was that of a wedding cake, frosted in dazzling white lights that had been strung throughout the branches of century-old oaks.

At least a half-dozen parking attendants sporting red blazers and looking like giant elves, popped in and out of a steadily arriving stream of vehicles. Antique gaslights flanked the steps that led to the house, and the banisters were elaborately garlanded with live holly and clusters of nuts and fresh fruit. Pots of brilliant red and white poinsettias were arranged along the illuminated walkway to the front door.

A doorman in white gloves and tails opened the door as they stopped. "Good evening and welcome."

Veretha took his hand as she exited the limo. She moved with the grace of a model, and Kathryn felt positively gawky by comparison, especially when her short black dress rode up her thighs as she slid across the seat and stepped out.

Devlin followed, stopping at her side and taking her arm in his. "I trust you'll have an enjoyable time tonight."

"I don't see how I can miss. It looks like quite a gala."

"Grace Tujacque traditionally hosts a holiday party the first weekend in December. For many it's considered the beginning of the Christmas social season. The guest list will read like a New Orleans who's who." Devlin released her arm but walked at her side as they climbed the steps.

Another couple approached, the woman in a floor-length, sequined gown, diamonds dripping from her ears. "I'm not sure I'm dressed for the occasion," Kathryn whispered.

"You look very elegant. I'm sure you'll get more than your share of attention, but save some time for me. I'd love to show you Grace's garden."

"I'd like that very much." In fact, she planned to spend as much time as possible with Devlin tonight. With luck, he'd have a few drinks, lose some of his practiced control, let his tongue slip and release a few secrets.

Roark had stepped in for Devlin, linking his arm with Veretha's as they climbed the steps. Another of his job requirements, Kathryn suspected. Keep Veretha company while Devlin lined up new prospects. If so, it appeared to be a task he enjoyed. Veretha rose on tiptoe to whisper something in his ear, and he smiled broadly. The action irritated her. The fact that she cared what the two of them did irritated her even more.

Grace Tujacque met them at the door, dressed in a dazzling red dress that fit high around the neck, fell loose over her stout figure and stopped just short of her high-heeled silver sandals. It was difficult to tell her age. There were few wrinkles in her face and neck, probably all pulled tight through numerous plastic surgeries, but her hands, arms and voice suggested she was likely in her late sixties or early seventies.

She greeted them with a warm smile and a welcoming hug for Devlin. When Devlin kissed her on the cheek, she glowed like a schoolgirl. Unbelievable, Kathryn thought. The man collected admirers like a kid might collect stamps. All ages. All types. From anywhere and everywhere.

She tried to imagine him locking any of them away

in a dark barred room, the way she'd imagined he'd done with Lisa. The picture wouldn't come into focus now that she'd met the man and seen him in action, especially here, smiling and looking like a polished aristocrat. But then, even the devil himself could probably play a gentleman if it suited his purposes.

Once they'd passed through the foyer, Devlin left her side to join Veretha, and Roark fell in step beside her. The two men made an incredible team. Something for everyone. Mostly for themselves.

She took in the sights and sounds of the party. A tall, stately fir tree stood in the middle of the room, heavily flocked with fake snow, and decorated with gold balls, iridescent ribbon and exquisite angels. A bespeckled, gray-haired man sat at the grand piano in the corner of the room playing Christmas songs, and servants scurried about serving drinks and passing around trays of hors d'oeuvres. "This is quite a soiree," she commented.

"If you like opulence," Roark replied.

"I take it you don't."

He stuck a finger under his black bow tie, wiggling it loose from his neck. "I'd like it better if I could breathe."

"Men. You always want everything," she teased.

"But we usually settle for much less. What about you, Kathryn? Something tells me you never settle for less than perfection, at least not from yourself."

His insight amazed her, but she didn't give him the satisfaction of admitting he was right.

She scanned the rest of the room, awed not only by the elaborate decorations but by the antique furnishings. "If it weren't for the party atmosphere, I'd feel as if I were in a museum. Every piece of furniture looks like a priceless antique.''

''I'm sure that's so. Both Mr. and Mrs. Tujacque descended from old money and they managed to add to their legacy. Mr. Tujacque opened a chain of department stores that became successful all over the South, then sold them a few years before his death for enough money to pay off the national debt.''

''You're surely exaggerating.''

''Only slightly.''

A waiter passed them carrying a tray of pastry-wrapped shrimp. She took one. Roark took several. She popped hers into her mouth, chewed slowly, reveling in a taste of crispy coconut, spicy shellfish and flaky crust. By the time she'd finished her one, Roark had finished all of his.

''Would you like a tour of the house?'' he asked, wiping his mouth and fingers on the dainty cocktail napkin that had come with the canapé.

''I'd love one. Have you been here before?''

''A few times, though only when Devlin brought me along with him. I'd never rate an invitation on my own. I'm merely the keeper of the shop, you know.''

''It seems you're much more than that. I get the impression that Devlin depends on you for a lot of things.''

''I understand and appreciate his work and his doctrine. He knows he can count on me to do what's needed.''

''That must mean a lot to him.''

''Devlin has many people he can count on, Kathryn, and many friends. I consider myself fortunate to be among them. Let's get a drink, and then I'll show you the second floor of the house. Mrs. Tujacque has one room filled with dolls she's collected from all over the world.''

"I'd love to see that.''

"Then what will it be? A cocktail or more champagne?''

"I'd like a club soda with a twist of lime.''

"Can't get much wallop from that.''

Which was why she was sticking to it. This might be a party for everyone else here tonight, but it was an investigative mission for her. "I'm not much of a drinker.''

"Neither am I, but I'll need more than club soda to get me through this night.''

She waited while he went for the drinks. The night was early, but the room they were in was already crowded with couples and small clusters of people, everyone dressed to the nines. The elite of New Orleans, all gathered in one spot. This had to be a dream situation for a con man like Devlin. So many pockets just waiting to be picked, so to speak.

But tonight *she* was obviously his target. Why else would he have invited her here except to impress her and to decide if she was worth a further investment of his time?

This was probably the exact same way he'd started with Lisa, laying on the charm, seducing her with his attention and charisma. Seducing her and convincing her to cut off all relations with her family a few short weeks before she received her trust fund. And now she'd disappeared completely.

Kathryn shivered, once again feeling a chill that reached deep inside her, a dread that cut off her breath.

Mrs. Tujacque walked by and stopped, obviously reading her distraught look as the result of being abandoned. "I can't believe Devlin and Roark have left you all alone."

"I'm fine. Just admiring your beautiful home."

"Still, I can't believe those men. Come with me. I know someone who'd love to meet you."

Kathryn started to explain that Roark had just gone for drinks, but changed her mind as she followed her hostess across the room.

"Roger could definitely use a little of your charm."

"That's nice of you to say." Though at the moment she didn't feel charming at all. Fearful, apprehensive, nervous. But not charming.

"Roger's a grouch, but he does have a few good qualities. Mainly he's smart like his dad was, God rest his soul. Unfortunately he has the temperament of a Hun."

"Is Roger your son?"

"Yes, that's him standing over there by the fern, looking bored."

Kathryn spotted the man. He was about six-two, not thin, not fat, though he did have the beginnings of a paunch. Rather nondescript, considering the flamboyancy of his mother. But Kathryn would describe his impression as more annoyed than bored. His face looked as if his skin might crack if he tried to smile.

Mrs. Tujacque took her arm as they approached him. "I have someone I'd like you to meet, Roger. This is Kathryn..."

"Richards," Kathryn supplied.

"Kathryn's a friend of Devlin Tisch."

"My condolences," he said, the frown never leaving his face.

"Be nice, Roger," his mother coaxed.

"Why? If Kathryn's here with Devlin Tishe, she's

already being drowned in niceness. A little brusque honesty will be a novelty for her.''

Mrs. Tujacque shook her head, her silvery curls sprayed into place so well that not a hair moved. She turned to Kathryn. ''Don't feel you have to put up with him any longer than you like, dear. I'm afraid I've failed miserably in teaching him any manners.''

Roger leaned over and gave his mother a kiss on the cheek. ''You did your best. Now go enjoy your splendid party.''

''It is festive, isn't it? Everyone seems to be having such a marvelous time, and not one of the caterers or florists let me down.''

She walked away, beaming.

''You're a brave one,'' Roger said. ''Usually I manage to frighten away Mother's guests in under ten seconds.''

''If you don't like her friends, why do you come to her parties?''

''To see what new and inventive ways she's found to squander money. An amazing talent she has. I'm constantly awed by it.''

''It's her money, isn't it?''

''Yes, and she has more than she can spend in a lifetime, thanks to the fact that Dad had the foresight to leave me in control of her investments. So, I'm just a Scrooge. What can I say?''

''She does throw a magnificent party.''

''The hostess with the mostess. She lives for this sort of thing, at least she did before she met up with your buddy Devlin.''

''What is it she lives for now?''

''Speaking with my dearly departed father, of

course. For a quiet man, he's become amazingly talkative now that he's dead.''

"You mean Devlin puts her in touch with your dad?''

"You sound surprised. I thought you were his friend. Surely you're aware that channeling is among his many talents.''

"I'm more familiar with his doctrine on harmony of the spirits.''

"Then you have a lot to learn. The man's a walking, talking spiritual miracle worker. I expect the Virgin Mary to make an appearance at Mystic Isle any day now. Perhaps for Christmas.'' He leaned in close as if he was sharing a secret with her. "Better save your money. Considering what it costs just to speak with dear old Dad, you'll probably have to sell that bauble around your neck to get your chance with the Virgin.'' Even at a whisper, Roger's voice burned with caustic sarcasm.

Kathryn reeled under the new information. Channeling explained the number of older wealthy women she'd seen at Mystic Isle. It could also be one more reason Devlin had gotten such a hold on Lisa. If he had her believing he could get her in contact with their parents, she'd have even more reason to hand over everything she owned.

"So if Devlin doesn't contact the dearly departed, what does he do for you?'' Roger asked.

"Nothing. I've only known him a short time.''

"In that case, take my advice and keep your wallet closed tight.''

"He seems a very honest man,'' Kathryn lied.

"Could be. Besides, it's your dollar. No reason to listen to a cynic like me.''

"No, I'd like to hear more."

"Too late. Your buddy Dev has spotted you with me and is rushing to your rescue as we speak."

She didn't turn around, but acknowledged Devlin's greeting as he walked up, then waited while the two men made small talk that seemed friendly enough on the surface, barbed if you paid attention to the nuances.

"If you'll excuse us, Roger, I've promised to show Kathryn your mother's garden."

"That should be a real treat for her." His tone and expression made it obvious he didn't believe the sentiment.

"I'm sure it will be. Your mother puts such care into her gardening and decorating." Devlin put a hand at the small of Kathryn's back as he guided her into the next room and toward a large door that opened to the west veranda. "How did you end up with Roger Tujacque?"

"His mother introduced us. He definitely lacks her charm."

"That he does. I'm sorry you got stuck with him. I feel remiss in my duty to make sure you have an enjoyable time tonight."

"You shouldn't think of me as a duty."

"I don't." He escorted her through the door, across the porch and down another set of steps. The December air was brisk, but dozens of people had spilled out onto the lawn where white tents had been set up and filled with chairs and tables covered in white cloths.

She scanned the area for Roark. It worried her that he'd never come back looking for her, but it was a large party. He could have just gotten involved with another of their followers.

Devlin slipped an arm around her waist as he led her

away from the guests and down a brick walkway lined with luminarias. The flickering light from the candles created dancing shadows on the translucent bags. They walked slowly amid beds of yellow mums, purple pansies, multicolored snapdragons and several varieties of plants Kathryn didn't recognize, all fragrant and growing in riotous profusion in the warm, humid climate of southern Louisiana. The sounds of Christmas music drifted from the party, joining but not overriding the babbling of a large garden fountain.

"The whole garden is lovely," she said, stopping to admire a bronzed statue of two children playing leapfrog, lit by a strategically placed spotlight. "The sights and the sounds."

"I thought you'd like it."

"It reminds me of your lecture the other night," she said, striving to appear genuinely interested in him and his work while digging for information. "The garden is a model of peace, beauty and harmony."

"You're right. When I walk here with Grace, I realize how closely it reflects her emotional, intellectual and spiritual growth over the last eighteen months."

"Is that when you met her? Eighteen months ago?"

"Yes. She came to us, devastated by her husband's unexpected death."

"She must miss him very much."

"She did at first, especially since their last morning together had been spent in a meaningless argument. Now she knows that he has forgiven her."

"How does she know that?"

"Communing with the spirits is not a one-way street, Kathryn. They not only listen to us, they speak to us, and in rare instances allow the living to communicate with the dead. It happens only rarely, however, and usually there must be a facilitator.''

''I've heard of channeling, but I've never met a person who could do it.'' She was certain she still hadn't, but for the first time, she had the feeling she was actually getting somewhere.

''Is there someone you'd like to contact?'' Devlin asked.

She hesitated, knowing she'd have to back up her request with reasonable lies. ''I'd love to speak to my great-grandmother. She died when I was a baby, and all my life I've felt drawn to her. I think she's trying to tell me something, but my family has always discredited my feelings about that.''

''People frequently discredit what they don't understand, but in truth it can actually be dangerous not to try and make contact with someone who is reaching out to you from the spiritual realm. The dead may still have needs that must be satisfied before they can rest in peace.''

The breeze gusted, quick and cold, and Kathryn shivered and wrapped her arms around herself. She didn't believe a word of what Devlin was saying, and yet she had the bizarre feeling that someone was indeed trying to tell her something. Maybe Lisa. But, please dear God, not from the dead. Maybe Raycine Ranklin, because all of a sudden Kathryn was consumed with the feeling that she had been here, in this same spot, with Devlin—or with Roark.

''You're shivering. Here, why don't you wear my coat?''

She met his gaze and prayed he couldn't read the fear that had taken hold of her again. ''I couldn't do that.''

"Of course you can, my dear." He slipped out of the tuxedo jacket and wrapped it around her shoulders, letting his hands linger at the base of her neck to hold it in place. "The spirits are speaking to me, Kathryn. They want me to help you."

"The spirits frighten me, Devlin. I wouldn't know how to begin to contact my great-grandmother."

"I do, but it's not easy. It takes so much of my concentration that it leaves me totally drained, sometimes physically ill. And it doesn't always work, at least not the first time. For Grace we had to travel back into the spirit world again and again before she was able to close the gap that separated her from her late husband. For others the process works quickly."

And what about Lisa? How long did it take you to make her believe in your bogus powers? She ached to scream the question at him. Instead, she worked to keep her voice steady. "Tell me about the process, Devlin. What would I have to do?"

He led her to a white garden bench beneath the bare limbs of a birch tree. He motioned her to sit and then sat beside her, taking both her hands in his. "This would be a big step for both of us, Kathryn, one I don't usually make with people until I know them well." His voice was mesmerizing, hypnotic, his hands gentle and reassuring. "It could be dangerous for us to move too quickly."

"Why is that, Devlin? What would make it dangerous?"

"It will bind us together, Kathryn. What you fear may become my fears. What touches me can touch you, unless I know so much about you that I can avoid the snares of spirits who would bring either of us evil."

His hesitancy seemed so real, his concerns so genuine. She took a deep, cleansing breath and struggled to remind herself that he was the evil one and that he had ensnared Lisa in his trap. "I can tell you everything there is to know about me."

"You would try, but you could only tell me the things you know. So many things are hidden deep in our subconscious. The only way it would be safe is if I were to hypnotize you, discover fears and truths that you've entombed in the deepest crevices of your memory."

Hypnotized. She'd never even thought of that, but of course, that would give him what appeared to be omniscient powers. He'd know things about people that they didn't necessarily remember or understand themselves. If he hypnotized her, he'd find out her true identity, know that she was Lisa's sister and that she'd come to Mystic Isle searching frantically for any clue as to her whereabouts.

She shook her head, this time letting her uneasiness come through. "I'm afraid of hypnotism. I could never consent to that."

"Well, without it, communing with your great-grandmother would be more difficult, but not necessarily impossible. But we would need to spend time together, quality time where you open up to me in a way you've likely never opened up to anyone. You'd have to trust me."

Trust Devlin Tishe. Trust the devil. Almost one and the same. "I'd like to trust you, Devlin, but I barely know you."

"I feel you've been disappointed by men before."

"Am I so obvious?"

"You're tender, gentle, yet afraid, Kathryn. I can take you to a place where you've never been before, a higher plane, give you experiences that will make you feel complete and totally secure, even if we don't contact your grandmother, but you must trust me.''

Take her places she'd never been before—like his bed. Or to private rooms behind the locked doors on the second floor of Mystic Isle where who knew what went on. Reality returned with painful clarity, and her flesh crawled at the prospect of his touch. Yet she had to get inside the inner circle, find out what happened to women who bought into his lies.

''How, Devlin? Just tell me how.''

He tucked a hand under her chin, tilted her face so that she met his gaze. ''First you must understand that I won't hurt you, that my touch is beyond the physical, that whatever passes between us is part of the spiritual union we must form in order for me to transport you through the veils of death without harm.''

Her blood ran cold. How easy it must be for him to sway the hearts of young innocent women. For money. For sexual favors. For anything he wanted. It was his knowledge and the mesmerizing quality of his voice that gave him the power, and yet he almost made her believe that he was more than a mortal.

''I trust you, Devlin.''

''Then you'll put yourself in my hands?''

''If that's what it takes.''

He touched his lips to hers, and she felt her insides recoil, her muscles cringe. So different from her response to Roark. Yet the two men were opposite sides of a worthless coin. So why did one fill her with such revulsion while the other dipped inside her like fingers of fire?

Voices drifted toward them, another couple who'd decided to view the gardens. Devlin pulled away from her. "We should go back inside now, but you must remember what we talked about. The trust must deepen. The bonds between us must grow stronger before the spirits will let me take you through the narrow passage. You do understand that this is all for you?"

"I understand. When do we start, Devlin?"

"Now, Kathryn. The spirits are already moving. I feel them inside me."

She trembled, fully aware of what he wanted from her. And of what she needed from him. But no matter how the spirits were moving him, as he put it, she wouldn't have to deal with him tonight. Veretha was with them and surely he'd go home with her.

VERETHA STOOD in the shadows watching Devlin with his newest recruit. He was touching her, staring into her eyes, thinking about what it would be like to make love to her. He was probably already arranging it for later tonight.

Only, he didn't need recruits any longer. Three more days and he'd have Lisa's money in his hands. They were supposed to go away together then. Leave the country. Start a new life. But it was all a lie. She should have known that from the very beginning. How could she have ever trusted a man whose whole life was built on illusions?

A curse echoed in her mind, and she could feel the sway of the power coming over her, almost as if she was back in her white robes, stroking her snakes, leading her people into the realm of the forbidden.

Devlin thought she needed him, that all she had were impotent potions and spells, curses and cures that she'd taught herself. But she held the real power and she wasn't afraid to use it. Though Devlin would realize that, he'd realize it too late.

Too late for Lisa Morland. Too late for Devlin and too late for the unfortunate woman who'd just become the latest victim of his charms.

Too late. Too late. Too late.

Chapter Ten

Roark stood by himself, a few yards from the back entrance to the Tujacque mansion, catching a breath of fresh air and a moment's relief from the constant chatter of rich socialites who enjoyed the attention of a younger, available man.

He'd planned to stay close to Kathryn tonight but she'd disappeared when he'd gone to get her a drink. The next time he saw her, she was walking out the side door with Devlin. The fact that they were alone together made him increasingly nervous. Devlin had a weakness for beautiful women, some might even call it an addiction, but he was still an intelligent and crafty man who did whatever it took to land on top.

One slip of the tongue on Kathryn's part, one tiny mistake, and Devlin would see right through the thin veneer of her facade. A lot of men would do everything *short* of murder for twelve million dollars. Unless he was seriously wrong about the man, Devlin had crossed that line long ago.

Kathryn was nowhere in sight, but Veretha was rushing down the brick walk, her shiny black hair flying in the slight wind, her usually calm and sensual face twisted into hard angry lines. Trouble, and he had the sickening feeling that it had to do with Kathryn and Devlin.

He hurried to catch up with her. "Is something wrong?"

Her hands flew to her shapely hips, and her eyes shot fire. "Yes. The same thing that is always wrong."

"You need to calm down and lower your voice."

"Don't tell me what I need, Roark Lansing. If you have advice you'd better give it to Devlin."

"Did he upset you?"

"Me? Upset? Where did you get an idea like that?"

He took her arm. "Let's go over to one of the tables near the bandstand. I'll get you a drink."

"I don't want a drink. If you want to do something, go with me right now. Take me to your apartment and make love to me. I'm a woman with needs like any other woman, and it's time someone realized that."

"You know I can't do that, Veretha." He tried to guide her away from the walk. She stood her ground.

"Of course you can't, Roark. You're too busy sucking up to Devlin, probably because you spend half your life covering up for him while he plays me for a fool."

"Devlin is just doing his job, Veretha." Roark kept his voice low, wishing she'd do the same. This was not the time or place for her to blow up. "You know how the operation works. He has to play up to the women."

"Playing up to them is one thing. Falling for them is another. First Raycine. Then Lisa. Now he's all over that snotty Kathryn he brought to the party tonight. And don't tell me it's for the money, Roark. Three more days and we're supposed to…" She stopped.

"Supposed to what, Veretha?"

"Ask Devlin. And while you're at it, tell him I'll find my own way home—when I'm good and ready."

"You can't just leave by yourself."

"Can't I? Watch me."

"Where are you going?"

"None of your business."

"What do you want me to tell Devlin?"

"You can tell him to go to hell."

She broke away from him and ran toward the front of the house, practically knocking over a waiter carrying a tray of filled champagne flutes, then continuing without bothering to apologize.

Desperation clawed inside Roark. Everything was falling apart. What he needed was a miracle.

What he got was another kick in the gut.

Kathryn and Devlin were walking down the path, side by side, their arms touching, their thighs occasionally brushing, looking for all the world like lovers. Devlin whispered something in her ear, and her lips parted in a wide smile. But they would have had to do more than touch and smile to have sent Veretha into the wildly spinning orbit she'd been in when she'd stormed away from the party.

He'd been so sure Kathryn was too smart to fall for the likes of Devlin, convinced himself that she knew what she was doing. But he was the fool. Devlin was the master. He couldn't be certain Kathryn's behavior wasn't just an act, but he had a sinking sensation in the pit of his stomach.

He had a message for Devlin and then he was cutting out. Kathryn could fall all over Devlin if that was what she wanted, but he wasn't staying around to watch the show.

KATHRYN STOOD between Devlin and Roark, sensing a tension between the two men that hadn't been there earlier. Roark stared at Devlin but ignored her completely. She couldn't really blame him for being upset with her. He'd gone for drinks. She'd disappeared with Devlin.

"I didn't mean to run out on you earlier," she said, feeling the need to apologize. "Mrs. Tujacque came over and wanted me to meet her son. I thought I'd see you when you came back, but I lost you in the crowd."

"No problem. It's a party. Mingling with new people is part of the fun."

His manner was the temperature of chipped ice, and he didn't bother to look at her when he spoke.

Devlin glanced around the room. "Have you seen Veretha?"

"As a matter of fact, I have," Roark answered. "She gave me a message to give you. Said to tell you she was leaving the party and that she'd see you at home— eventually."

"And that was it?"

"Pretty much. Actually I think I'm going to cut out, too, Devlin. I'm just not in much of a party mood tonight."

"You can't go!" Kathryn blurted before she thought. If he did, that would leave only Devlin to take her home. She'd be alone with him in the back of the limo, alone with him when they reached the hotel...

Finally Roark looked at her, his dark eyes holding her, tormenting her with their mysterious depths. She should be every bit as afraid of being alone with him as she was with Devlin, but it wasn't fear that rocked her when she met his gaze. It was an inexplicable bond, as if they were both drowning in the same riptide and needed each other to keep from going under.

Devlin dropped a hand to her shoulder. "Of course

he can go if he wants to, Kathryn. I'll see that you get home safely.''

"Actually I just meant he shouldn't leave by himself. He can drop me off at the hotel and you can stay and enjoy the party. It's been a busy day and I'm afraid I'm not much of a party animal.''

"I'd hoped we could talk more intimately about communing with the spirits, but we'll go whenever you're ready, Kathryn. I just need to spend a few minutes discussing business with Roark and then we'll find Grace and say our goodbyes.''

She couldn't think of any logical reason to protest. She hoped Roark would provide one, but he just stared past both of them as if he was already wasting his time discussing the matter. "What kind of business do we need to discuss, Devlin?''

"Just a little matter that came up tonight. I'll walk to the door with you if Kathryn doesn't mind waiting here for a few minutes.''

"I hope you have better luck than I did,'' Roark said. "I left her alone for a few minutes and you saw what happened to me.''

"I'll be waiting when you come back,'' Kathryn said, reacting to Roark's taunt. One minute she felt an attraction so strong she felt as if her feet weren't touching the floor. The next he had her seething. All this for a man who shouldn't affect her at all.

She was in over her head, but it was too late to turn back now. She had to find Lisa before...

Before the warning came true. Had to find her even if it meant facing Devlin Tishe alone tonight.

DEVLIN WAITED until he and Roark had exited the front door and were well out of earshot of other guests. It would all be over in a few days, but until then he had an image to uphold. "Did Veretha see Kathryn and me together?"

"That would be my guess. It was definitely you she was mad at. You must have given her a lot to see."

"A harmless kiss."

"Apparently Veretha didn't see it quite that way."

"I don't know what's gotten into her lately. She was so jealous of Raycine for a time there that I thought she was going to make me kick her out of the manor."

"Looking back, that might have been a good decision—especially for Raycine."

"Hindsight is always twenty/twenty. I'd like you to investigate Kathryn Richards's background for me."

More fun. "I thought that was Lisa's job."

"It was. She's been relieved of that duty."

"Why's that?" But Roark already knew the answer. Someone had disconnected and removed the modem from the computer at Tujacque's Manor, cutting off Lisa's access to the outside world. One more way to make sure she didn't find out about Raycine's murder before her birthday.

"Lisa was having so much difficulty with the investigations that I've decided to do them from Mystic Isle the way I used to before Raycine took them over for me."

"It should be a simple investigation. I'll get on it tomorrow. In the meantime I'd go easy with Kathryn Richards. She seems a little more sophisticated than the ones we usually get."

"She is. Sophisticated, smart, beautiful."

"Are you looking for a challenge?"

"That's part of it."

"And the other part?"

"I like her, Roark. I really do. There's a quality about her you don't see every day. Strong, yet soft, the kind of woman who could satisfy all of a man's needs, not just his physical ones."

So Devlin was actually falling for Kathryn. Veretha had been right on target. This did complicate the mix. "Is there anything else, Devlin?"

"There is one other thing. I've heard from a reliable source that Veretha is playing at being a voodoo priestess again and that she's holding a meeting in Algiers tomorrow night. If she does, I want to know about it and I want all the details, straight and unbiased. I know I can count on you for that."

"So you want me to follow her?"

"I know she's already asked you to go with her. I want you to say yes. A man in my position can't afford to have his wife dancing around with her snakes in public and presiding over ritualistic, heathen meetings where drug use runs rampant. If word of that got out, it could destroy all I've worked for."

And if he knew that Veretha had asked him to go to the meeting with him, he also knew that she'd come on to Roark. He'd always suspected that the offices at Mystic Isle were bugged. This just gave credence to his suspicion. Fortunately for him, he'd turned down her advances.

"Anything else?" Roark asked.

"I think that covers it."

Check out the background for Devlin's new girlfriend and spy on the man's wife. It was a great job he'd gotten himself into. Only, he didn't need to spy on Kathryn. He knew all there was to know about her, right down to the salty-sweet taste of her when her tongue slipped between his lips. But he'd leave that out of the report. Actually he'd leave everything he actually knew about Kathryn out of the report. It shouldn't take him more than an hour to make up one that Devlin would like.

Truth was, he'd go down to Mystic Isle and do that right now. He was in no mood for going back to his empty apartment. No mood to imagine Kathryn with Devlin.

Tell my sister I'm safe.

Lisa's request echoed in his mind as he climbed into the taxi. Perhaps it would have been better if he'd told Kathryn the truth about everything. He'd tried to tell himself he was protecting Lisa and Kathryn, but maybe he had turned into a man no better than Devlin himself. The need for revenge had driven him for months. Now it was turning sour inside him.

It was too late to save Margie. All he could do now was try to make sure Devlin didn't kill again. He'd planned to go to Mystic Isle, but when the driver asked for his destination, he told him the Pontchartrain Hotel.

BY THE TIME the limousine pulled up in front of the hotel, Kathryn had gone over a dozen plans in her mind, rejecting them one by one. She needed to talk to Devlin, had to find a way to get information out of him, but she was becoming ill at the thought of having him in her hotel room, of having him touch her or kiss her the way he had in Mrs. Tujacque's garden.

Why hadn't she just hired a new investigator when the first one didn't seem to be getting anywhere? She surely could have found someone who could have tracked Lisa down. Now it was too late. *Dead before her birthday.*

The threat had seemed frightening in Dallas, but not

totally real. More like a hoax, a bad joke, the kind some of Lisa's old friends might have pulled. But here in New Orleans, mixed up in a world of spirits and channeling and men like Devlin Tishe, it seemed all too genuine. It was reality now that appeared to be the illusion. And still, she couldn't let Devlin in her room.

"I'm really tired tonight, Devlin. I'd hoped we could talk, but I don't think I'm up to it."

"Are you afraid of me, Kathryn? You needn't be."

"It's not that. I've had this headache for days. It comes and goes, but right now it's beginning to pound again." She rubbed her temples, realizing she was telling the truth.

He put his hands on her neck and began to massage, running his fingers down the corded muscles and digging them into the flesh of her shoulders. "You're very tight."

She pulled away. "I know, but I just need to rest. I'm sorry, Devlin. I'd like to come into your office tomorrow and talk about my trying to contact the spirit of my great-grandmother, but I can't talk anymore tonight."

"Yes, tomorrow." He motioned to the chauffeur. The driver climbed out and opened the door for them. "But I'll still walk you to your door."

The hotel lobby was crowded. Kathryn dodged the people, not slowing until she stepped into a waiting elevator. She was only vaguely aware of Devlin's hand on her arm. Her mind had already slipped back to earlier tonight when Roark had stepped inside her door, two flutes of champagne in hand, and knocked the rug right out from under her.

She had no more reason to trust Roark than anyone else at Mystic Isle, yet she felt drawn to him in a way that defied reason. She longed for him to be beside her now. Time was running out, and she had to trust someone if she was ever going to find Lisa and make certain she was safe.

Devlin rode the elevator with her. She lingered when it stopped at her floor. She didn't want him at her door, didn't want him inside her room.

"Go back to Veretha, Devlin. I'll be fine."

"I'd like to see you inside your room, Kathryn."

"No. The hotel's crowded. Keep the elevator while it's here." She read the hesitancy in his eyes. "Please, Devlin. We can talk tomorrow, but tonight I just want to rest."

"If you insist."

"I do."

And with that, he was gone, leaving Kathryn alone with her thoughts.

ROARK STOOD in the doorway of the lounge after he'd watched Kathryn walk by on Devlin's arm. The idea of Devlin taking advantage of Kathryn made his stomach pitch. This was all his fault. In trying to protect Lisa and Kathryn, he'd kept his mouth shut and let Kathryn succumb to Devlin's polished charm. For all he knew, she might trust him so completely by now that she'd told him who she really was.

And no matter how attractive Devlin might find Kathryn, he'd never give up Lisa's millions. Roark walked to the staircase and took the steps to the fifth floor. He didn't know what Devlin would say when he showed up at the door. And right now he didn't much care.

All he knew was that he wasn't going to stand by and do nothing. Adrenaline was pumping through him, pushing him almost to a run as he reached the last turn in the stairwell. A few seconds later he pushed through the door and into the fifth-floor hallway. Kathryn's room was at the other end.

Before he reached it, he heard a bloodcurdling scream. He froze for a fraction of a second and then took off at a run, certain the scream had been hers.

Chapter Eleven

Kathryn stared, paralyzed with fear. The room was alive, overflowing with the slithering, squirming, coiling movements of hideous black snakes.

This wasn't happening, couldn't be real. It was a nightmare, and if she opened her eyes, it would go away. Only, her eyes were open, and the snakes were still there, in the curtains, under the chair, on the dresser.

And a tangle of slithering, tongue-flicking reptiles, were thrashing in the middle of her bed, in and out of the sheets, on top of and under the pillows, sliding onto the floor. And someone, somewhere was screaming.

The door flew open and she turned, unable to think, afraid the nightmare would only worsen.

"Oh, my, God!"

It was Roark, standing in her doorway, his gaze fixed on the bed. She tried to call out to him, but her voice only rose in a shrill cry. One of the snakes was crawling across her foot. She kicked it away, but felt something wrap around her leg, caught a glimpse of black as it slid up her thigh.

Roark grabbed the snake, yanked it from her leg and tossed it across the room. He was talking to her, but his words didn't register in her frenzied mind. He grabbed her arm and pulled her out the door into the hallway, slamming the door shut behind them.

Her screams had stopped, but she was crumbling, her body caving in, turning to a limp heap. Roark caught her in his arms and pulled her back to a standing position.

"It's okay, Kathryn. It's okay." He continued to hold her, though at least half the doors on the floor had been flung open and people had spilled into the hallway to stare.

"What the devil is going on out here?" a man growled.

"One of those giant cockroaches," Roark answered. "Scared her half to death. She's not from around here."

"You woke up the whole hotel for a cockroach?" The man looked at her as if she were some green alien from outer space.

Another woman, dressed in pajamas, her robe open, came over and patted Kathryn on the arm. "I know how you feel, honey. I did the same thing the first time I saw one of those things. I thought for sure I was going to have a heart attack." The others just shrugged, muttered under their breaths and went back into their rooms.

When Kathryn recovered from the shock enough to react, she pulled from Roark's arms. "There was no stupid cockroach. There are snakes everywhere, coming through the walls. I have to warn the other guests."

"The snakes aren't everywhere and they're not going to bother them. The snakes were a personal gift to *you*. And we're not staying around to explain." He tugged her toward the elevator. "You're in shock. Just walk and let me do the talking if there's any to be done."

"What are you doing?"

"Getting you out of here."

She stopped and held her ground. "And just leave the snakes?"

"I'm damn sure not taking them with us. But don't worry, I'll call security from my place. They'll take care of getting rid of them."

"How will they? There are so many of them." Her voice sounded strange, hoarse from her screams and shaky from the shudders that still shook her body, but this time she let herself be led to the elevator.

"The snakes aren't poisonous. They weren't meant to kill you, just to scare you to death."

"It almost worked." She was still struggling for a steady breath. "Who would do such a thing?"

"Only one person I can think of. Our Lady of the Snakes. Veretha Tishe."

The bell clanged and the elevator door slid open. A security guard stared at them. "Are you folks okay?"

"We're fine. My girlfriend did a little too much celebrating tonight, but she'll be okay when she sobers up."

The guard continued to stare at her, his hand riding the butt of the pistol on his hip. "Is that right, Miss?"

She nodded, not trusting her voice, still not able to think clearly or take control.

The guard continued to stare at her. "You sure you're all right?"

She could only imagine what she looked like, probably ashen, maybe green. She was beginning to feel really sick. She leaned against Roark, hoping to control her shaking. "I'm a little drunk."

"Well, someone reported screaming up here. Did you two hear anything?"

"Sure did. Some woman saw a cockroach and she was carrying on like a maniac," Roark said. "I think somebody finally squashed the damned thing for her."

The guard still didn't look convinced, but he finally stepped away from them and headed down the hall.

Roark kept his arm around her as the elevator door closed and they started the downward plunge. "Good going, Kathryn."

"I did what you asked, but I don't know why we needed to lie to the man. You could have told him about the snakes, made sure he didn't open the door and find them the way I did."

"If we had, we'd be stuck up there all night, trying to explain the unexplainable, filling out a police report, getting the third degree. I don't think you're up to that right now."

"I'm not sure I'm even up to breathing yet."

"You'll have to. That's one thing I can't take care of for you."

"Where are you taking me?"

"To my place. It's not nearly as luxurious as what you're used to back in Dallas, but it's snake free."

"I'll take it," she answered quickly, knowing she'd rather have gone off with Jack the Ripper than go back and face that room full of snakes. But she was glad it was Roark who'd come to her rescue.

It took a minute more for the full effect of his statement to sink in. "What makes you think I live in luxury or in Dallas?"

"Because I know who you are, *Kathryn Morland.*"

The statement stunned her, though it shouldn't have. It should have been clear to her from the outset that the Tishe organization was too well tuned not to have checked out every detail of Lisa Morland's life, and that would have included her family.

"Where is Lisa?"

"Just hold on. Let's get out of this hotel before we continue this discussion," he said as the elevator doors opened on the lobby. "Everyone will be staring at you, but try to walk and act normally."

"Why will they be staring?"

"Because right now you look like the walking dead."

"Falling into bed with hundreds of snakes does that to me."

"Dozens, not hundreds." He took her arm and led her through the lobby, and just as he'd said, she got lots of stares. She glued her gaze to her shoes until they'd cleared the door and Roark had asked the bellman to whistle for a cab.

"What is it you want?" she asked. "If it's money, I can get it. I just want Lisa released."

He leaned in close. "What the hell are you talking about?"

"I'm talking about Lisa. What have you and Devlin done with her?"

He dropped his arm from around her shoulders. "I haven't *done* anything with Lisa. So far no one has, and I'm trying as hard as I can to see that no one does. I was doing a lot better job of that before you came on the scene."

"If Lisa hasn't been kidnapped, where is she and why has she disappeared so completely?"

"She has poor taste in men, though from the looks of the way you were hanging all over Devlin tonight, I'd say it's a family trait."

A taxi pulled to the curb. The bellman opened the door, and Kathryn climbed in, scooting all the way to the other side while Roark tipped the attendant. The experience with the snakes had left her mind and body a tangled mess, and the turn of this conversation wasn't helping to clear up her thought processes.

She barely waited until he was inside and the cab door was closed before starting in on him. "No more games, Roark. I don't have the energy or the patience for them tonight. If you know who I am, then you know why I'm here, and you know all about my sister Lisa."

"We'll talk at my place, not in the cab."

Naturally he wouldn't confess anything in front of witnesses. She leaned back and closed her eyes. The snakes returned, slithering, cold, slimy. Crawling all over her. Her eyes flew open again and she shifted, drawing up as if she was cold.

Roark reached across the seat as if to take her hand, then seemed to think better of it. "I know what you're thinking, Kathryn. It isn't true."

His voice was low, but resonated with strength, the same kind of strength she'd felt when he'd walked through the door of her hotel room and torn the snake from her body.

"You're safe with me, Kathryn. That much I can promise you."

And for some strange reason, she *almost* believed him.

ROARK HAD NO IDEA exactly how he was going to handle the situation, but from the moment he'd heard Kathryn's scream, he knew that he had to do something different from what he'd been doing. When he'd found her in the hotel room, pale, shaking, frightened half out of her mind, he knew that he had to tell her at least part of the truth. There were a lot more dangerous things than snakes out there, and if she continued to hang out with Devlin or snoop around Mystic Isle, she might be hit with one of them.

He should have worked more quickly, gotten to Raycine sooner, found a way to spend more time at the plantation house where the confidential and incriminating records were stored in hidden, protected files.

He knew the day-to-day operations of Mystic Isle from top to bottom. Knew how the scams worked to get people to donate large sums of money for private sessions that would supposedly bring them harmony and happiness. Knew how Devlin investigated family backgrounds, mental stability and financial standing to determine whom he wanted to target for personal attention. Knew how the man used his technical and psychological skills to convince people that they were talking to the dead. Even knew how he managed Veretha with a delicate blend of lies and promises.

But all any of that proved was that Devlin was an extremely talented and successful con artist. If convicted on those charges, he might spend a few years in jail, but then again, probably not. The jails were overcrowded with killers, armed robbers and rapists. Men like Devlin usually waltzed right by a parole board, had his sentence reduced in record time.

And that was *if* they got convicted. Before you reached that stage, a prosecuting attorney had to produce witnesses willing to admit they'd been taken in by the scams. A lot of Devlin's victims didn't even realize they were being taken. Then, too, Devlin would probably hold as much sway over a jury as he did over everyone else. Any way you looked at it, with no more evidence than Roark had, Devlin would likely never do a day of jail time.

But murder was a different matter. And a murder conviction was what Roark was after. He unlocked the door and stood back while Kathryn stepped inside. "Don't expect much and you won't be disappointed."

"I don't care about your apartment. Right now, Lisa is my only concern."

"Then you can relax, at least for the time being. She's safe and well. She asked me to tell you that."

Kathryn gripped his arm. "Then you do know where she is. You've talked to her."

"Chatted with her today."

"What did she say when you told her I was here in New Orleans?"

"I didn't."

"Why not?"

"I thought it was safer if she didn't know."

"So you just play God and decide who should know what and when they should know it?"

"It's not like that."

"It seems that way to me. Take me to her."

"I can't do that."

"Because the spirits don't think it's time?"

"Because I promised your sister that I wouldn't tell you where she is."

"Lies and promises, secrets and games. You must really enjoy living life on the edge, you and Devlin Tishe, manipulating your world and everyone who steps into it."

"I'm not the manipulator, Kathryn. I know it looks as if I'm in this with Devlin, but I'm not. I can't explain all the details to you, but Lisa isn't a prisoner. She's where she wants to be by choice."

"I'd love to believe that, Roark. But I can't, not without a logical reason why I should."

"It's a long and complicated story."

"I've got all night and I'd like to every word of it."

"I was certain that you would." He walked to the kitchen and made a phone call to hotel security. When he'd hung up he pulled two wineglasses from the cabinet, then filled them both with cabernet.

He handed her one of the glasses before leading her to the sofa, sure she'd need it by the time he finished his story, if she didn't already. She fit herself between a couple of magazines. He picked them up and tossed them out of the way. "Sorry the place is such a mess. I wasn't expecting company."

"Neither was I, especially not ones that coiled and slithered and flicked their ugly tongues at me."

He sat beside her, still struggling with how much he should say—how much he *could* say and not have her rush out of here and go flying into the face of danger.

She sipped her wine. "You can start talking anytime."

"I'm trying to decide where to start."

"Start with Lisa, Roark. Tell me where she is. I don't care what you promised her. I have to know. I have a right to know."

Kathryn waited for the response to her question, her wariness level shooting upward as she read the hesitancy in Roark's actions. He folded some cluttered newspaper and moved it to the edge of the coffee table, then leaned back and propped his feet where the paper had been.

"You said I could trust you, Roark."

"Trust works both ways," he answered, still not looking at her. "You're a Johnny-come-lately to the show. Lisa and I are already neck-deep in fast-sinking quicksand.''

The familiar churning started in her stomach again. She was here in Roark's apartment, wanting to believe him, praying he'd told her the truth when he'd said Lisa was safe, but he was too slow to answer, too hesitant to talk. All signs he was still dealing in deception. Still, she had to hear him out. ''Who are you, Roark Lansing?''

He exhaled sharply and finally turned to face her. ''I'm an impostor just like you are, Kathryn, not at all the man I pretend to be once I step inside the walls of Mystic Isle.''

''Yet you've worked with Devlin for nine months, or was that a lie, too? Is everything I know about you a lie?''

''Pretty much, but the nine months is actually the truth. I didn't just accidentally hook up with him. My actions were all part of a plan. I started attending the lectures at Mystic Isle, even paid for a couple of attempts to communicate with my mother.''

''Did you?''

''I talked to her. I still do, but she's not dead. She lives in Atlanta. I watched and learned and played his game, pretending to believe every word out of his mouth. Fortunately he took a liking to me.''

''And he offered you a job running the shop?''

''Not right away. At first he had me running errands for him and performing various tasks around the Isle. I worked cheap. It was Veretha who first decided my talents were wasted. She said if she dressed and trained me right, I would be sexy and seductive enough to get the attention of some of the female visitors.''

Veretha's plan had certainly worked with her, Kathryn thought. From the first moment she'd walked into the shop and heard Roark speak, she'd been bombarded with sensual awareness. But it was more than his voice and appearance that attracted her now. He put out an undefinable magnetism that made her want to believe him, even after he'd just admitted that everything he'd told her before tonight had been a lie.

She sipped her wine slowly as he continued his bizarre tale of living two lives. In one, he'd played the role of a man totally immersed in the doctrine of Devlin Tishe. In the other, he was constantly digging for information, learning everything he could about how Devlin operated. He admitted he'd been at Mystic Isle the night Lisa attended her first meeting.

"She showed up wearing a pair of tight jeans and a loose-fitting sweater. Her hair was tousled from the wind, and the second she looked at you with those big expressive eyes of hers, you had the feeling you were looking at a fallen angel."

"That's Lisa."

"And Devlin was Devlin. He was hot for her from the very first night."

"That was probably the night she called me raving about him, telling me about this marvelous man she'd met."

"She was taken with him all right, and he with her. Veretha noticed it, too. She has an uncanny ability to tell whether his relations are all business or if he's truly attracted to or infatuated with a woman. It was clear he was crazy about Lisa, and it got worse as the days went by. He didn't even bother running an investigation on her, and this is a man who'd investigate his own mother if she came walking into Mystic Isle and looked as if she might have a little money stashed away somewhere.''

''Veretha couldn't have liked that.''

''Not in the least. She started hanging around all the time, went looking for Devlin whenever he was out of her sight for more than a few minutes. That didn't deter him a bit, so she started coming on to me. I'm sure she was hoping to make Devlin jealous, but he barely noticed.''

''Did you and Veretha…?''

''Did we have an affair? No way. I wasn't doing anything to risk evoking Devlin's ire. Besides, I knew her by then, and believe me, she's not my type.''

''She's beautiful.''

''So are some snakes, but I'm not going to willingly crawl into bed with one of them.'' He stretched and resettled, this time spreading his arms over the back cushions of the sofa.

''That can't be the end of the story.''

''The beginning of the end.''

''Why is that?''

''All of a sudden the situation took a dramatic turn. Veretha began catering to Lisa, even making certain that Lisa and Devlin had lots of time to spend together. I knew something was up, so I did my own investigation.''

''And found out about the trust fund?''

''Eleven-point-nine million to be paid in full on Lisa's twenty-fifth birthday. Obviously Devlin and Veretha had already gotten their hands on that bit of news.''

''Lisa probably volunteered it. She's always been way too trusting.'' Kathryn set her near-empty wineglass on the table, her fingers so tense it was a wonder she hadn't crushed the glass. "I'm sure Devlin has some plan for getting his hands on Lisa's money."

"I don't have a doubt in my mind," Roark agreed. "Evidently he needs her alive to get the money. So as long as you don't give Devlin or Veretha any reason to think you've come here to stop that transfer from taking place, she'll be safe until her birthday."

"And then?" Kathryn asked the question, but she didn't need to hear Roark's answer. She'd considered the possibility when the attorney had first told her that he hadn't believed the caller was Lisa. Knew it with even more certainty when she'd received the phone call saying that Lisa would die before her birthday unless someone got her out of *that place*.

"Tell me where she is, Roark. Please tell me where she is."

"I've already told you I can't do that."

"Is there some crazy rule you live by that says you have to control everything?"

"I threw away every rule I've ever followed, Kathryn. Trashed them nine months ago when I came here to investigate the workings of Devlin Tishe. Threw away a big part of myself along with them, at least what was left to discard."

His voice had changed, grown husky. He clenched and unclenched his fists, and the veins in his neck and face stood out as if he was about to go into battle. He stared at the wall in front of him, unblinking, his face blank, as if he'd slid back into another time.

She felt a strange need to touch him, but held back. Showing emotion with Roark had a way of backfiring on her. "What happened to change you so?"

"It's not important to the story."

"I'd say it's vitally important."

"Then you'll just have to work around it." He stood and looked toward the hallway. "There's only one bedroom. You take it. I'll take the couch."

"Not yet. I want to talk to Lisa, to hear for myself that she's all right. If you won't tell me where she is, at least give me that."

He grimaced. "It's past midnight."

All the more reason she needed to talk to her. It was only two days until Lisa's birthday, and Kathryn sensed she was getting through to him. "Please, Roark."

"Then let's make a deal. I let you talk to Lisa, you stay away from Mystic Isle and from Devlin Tishe for the next two days."

"I can't promise you that."

"Then you need to move, because you're sitting on my bed and I'm tired and through with talking."

"I have to talk to her."

"I gave you the proposition. All I'm asking is two days, Kathryn. After that you're free to do whatever you like."

In two days Lisa would be twenty-five. If she was being kept alive just long enough for someone to get their hands on the money, then two days could be too late for Kathryn to do anything to stop it.

"It comes down to trust, Kathryn. Am I the enemy or am I the man I say I am? Am I after Lisa's soon-to-be fortune, or am I working against the clock to protect her and you?"

Trust. But she had no reason to trust him except that he'd known who she was all along and he'd had ample opportunity to get rid of her and make sure she didn't interfere with his plans. He could have dropped her in the bayou, let her wash up the way Raycine Ranklin had. He could have left her to the snakes. She struggled with the decision, then wondered why she was worrying about keeping a promise to a man who'd just admitted he'd lied to her from the first moment they'd met.

She wasn't back in Dallas with the people she knew. She'd entered a world of illusion that didn't seem to spin on the same axis as the one she'd known before. "Okay, Roark. Two days. Now let me talk to my sister."

Roark picked up his cell phone. "Just one thing you should remember when you talk to her."

"What's that?"

"She's in love with Devlin Tishe, or at least the man she thinks he is. She trusts him far more than she trusts either of us. The best thing you can do for her is not to mention him at all."

He punched in the number and handed her his phone. "She'll be asleep."

"Then she can wake up. I have to talk to her now."

Chapter Twelve

"Hello?"

Combers of relief swept through Kathryn at the sound of the familiar voice. She'd told herself all along that Lisa was alive, but she realized now how much doubt had existed deep inside her. "Lisa. It's me, Kathryn."

"Hi, sis. What's doing in dazzling Dallas?"

It was Lisa's customary greeting when things were going well between them. It eased the tension a tad, but not enough that Kathryn didn't still feel as if she was forcing the air into her lungs.

"Not a lot doing in Dallas. How are you?"

"Hanging in here. It's been a while. Guess you noticed, huh?"

"I noticed. I guess I woke you."

"No. I couldn't sleep. I was lying here staring at the ceiling. Roark Lansing must have called you."

"We've talked. He says you're safe and well, but I wanted to hear it from you." She hesitated, trying to imagine where Lisa was and if she was really all right. "It's good to hear your voice."

"Same here. I wanted to call you, Kathryn, started to a hundred times, especially Thanksgiving Day."

"Why didn't you?"

"Things are kind of up in the air around here. I was waiting until I could give you some good news."

"What kind of news?"

"I can't tell you now, but expect me one day soon to show up in Dallas and knock on your front door."

"I'm not in Dallas, Lisa. I'm in New Orleans." The silence lasted so long Kathryn was afraid Lisa had broken the connection.

"I hope you're not here because of me, Kathryn."

"Your phone was disconnected. The last two checks came back as undeliverable. I haven't heard from you in over a month. Of course I'm here because of you. I'd like to see you."

"I know. I'd like to see you, too. But I can't, not yet."

"I can visit you wherever you are."

"No. That's not a good idea, either."

"Please, Lisa. I know we've never been all that close, but I'm so worried about you. Why can't you tell me where you are? Why can't I see you?"

"How much did Roark tell you?"

"Not much." Not nearly enough. "If you're in some kind of trouble, I can help you."

"You can help, Kathryn, by staying out of this. There's something I have to do, and I have to do it by myself. When I've finished, I'll come to Dallas and tell you everything. In the meantime, just go home. If you try to track me down, you'll ruin everything. Do you understand?"

"I'm trying."

"Good. Now please, just go back to Dallas. I know you don't think I can take care of myself. I've never given you any reason to think I could, but I've learned a lot in the last few months. I'm finally growing up. You'll see.''

Growing up, but would she live to grow old? ''If you change your mind about seeing me, you can call me back.''

''I won't change my mind, Kathryn. Not until it's time. But when I see you, I'll have a great surprise.'' Silence again. ''I better go now.''

Kathryn's throat grew tight. ''I'm here if you need me.''

''God, don't I know it. You always have been. Don't know why you've put up with me this long.'' Lisa's voice cracked on the last few words, as if she was about to cry. ''Gotta go.''

''I love you,'' Kathryn whispered, trying to remember the last time she'd said that.

''I love you, too.'' The phone clicked and the connection went dead.

Most of Kathryn's questions were still unanswered when she handed the phone back to Roark. She didn't know where Lisa was or what she was doing. But she was safe and alive and that would have to do for now. ''Thanks, Roark.''

He wrapped his arm around her shoulders. This time his touch was different. She was still aware of him from her head to her toes, still felt the heat seep into her, but the edgy tinge of mistrust had lessened.

''Did Lisa tell you where she was?'' he asked.

''No, and she wouldn't agree to see me, but at least I know she's safe for now.''

''I plan to do everything in my power to keep her that way, Kathryn.''

''Then can't you make her just leave Devlin Tishe and go back to Dallas with me?''

"She's a grown woman. She has to make her own decisions about which risks are worth taking, the same way you do. The same way I do."

"Devlin Tishe is not worth any kind of risk. Surely she can see that."

"Not yet, but I think that day is coming soon."

"I just don't want it to come too late."

She leaned back, feeling tired and worn and years older than she had at this time last week. The wine was having its effect, making her eyelids heavy. But if she closed them, she might see snakes, and she didn't want that image in her mind again. She forced herself to concentrate on the positive. She'd talked to Lisa, heard her voice. She was alive and safe—for now.

The image went blank, then came back in living color, meshed with snakes and bodies being pulled out of murky water. And presiding over the hideous nightmare were Devlin and Veretha Tishe.

Kathryn felt crushed, as if hundreds of pounds of weight were being piled on her chest. She had to push them off, had to fight to save everybody. Only, she couldn't move, couldn't talk. All she could do was scream.

But then Roark appeared and the whole hideous picture faded away, all but Roark. He opened his arms and she stepped inside them. Finally someone had saved her.

December 6

BUTCH RANKLIN stepped from behind the shadows of a building at St. Ann and Royal streets. He wasn't sure of the time, didn't much care. He never slept anymore, not since Raycine's body had been found. It was probably close to 3:00 a.m. The streets in the French Quarter were practically deserted, most of the revelers from out-of-town having already returned to their hotel rooms.

The *weers* were out now—that's what they called them down at the station house. Like a lot of words coined in New Orleans, it was simply the running together of two words, the wee-hours folk, the people who didn't get off work until the restaurants and other late-night spots closed.

They roamed the streets until sunrise, surprisingly didn't cause all that much trouble, just men and women running on a different clock. Cops were a lot like that. You changed shifts, but your body didn't. Or else you were on a case that wouldn't let go of you just because it was bedtime.

He wasn't on Raycine's case. It was against department policy for a homicide detective to head up a case he was personally involved in. But all the cops knew that it didn't matter what the officials said or did, Butch was *on* this case. On it twenty-four hours a day.

He didn't know how his wife coped, but she was doing a hell of a lot better job than he was. She had her prayer group, her friends, her family. It didn't make up for the loss of Raycine—nothing ever would—but she managed. All Butch had was guilt and grief, and he wasn't coping. He merely survived on determination and the same old force that drove every cop worth his measly paycheck.

He'd get his man.

"Pssst."

He spun around at the sound, his hand already on the butt of his piece. A slim figure moved in the shadows. He grabbed his flashlight and shot a beam of illumination into the doorway.

A girl cringed and covered her face. "Detective Ranklin."

"That's me." The girl looked like half the punks on the street these days. Dyed-red hair, cropped off at all kinds of weird angles, dirty torn jeans, filthy shoes. It took him a few seconds to realize that he'd met her before.

"Do you remember me?" she asked.

"Don't recall your name, but I ran into you down here one night with my daugh—" His throat closed and he didn't quite get the word out. "Punch," he said, pulling the name from somewhere in his mind. "Raycine called you Punch."

"That's right."

He stepped closer. "I guess you heard she's dead."

"I heard. I keep thinking about it—about her. She was a real nice person. She hung out with us, but she wasn't like us. She was just exploring the world and we were part of it."

"Yeah." He leaned against the door frame. "I'm exploring her world right now, Punch. Somebody in it killed her, and that somebody needs to be locked away before he kills again. Might be you next time, or one of your other friends."

"I know."

The teenager not only knew, but was as scared as a rabbit in a den of foxes. He could read people like a book. That was what made him a good detective. "Talk to me, Punch. Give me a name, a place to start looking."

She stared at the toes of her shoes.

"Did Raycine make somebody mad? Somebody have it in for her?"

She stuffed her hands in her pockets, digging down deep, but kept her gaze on her feet.

"Help me out here, Punch. Where was she hanging out? Who wanted her dead?"

Still nothing, but she wanted to talk or she wouldn't have called him over. Poor scared kid. "No one will ever know I heard it from you. And if you ever need a favor, I'm your man."

Punch finally looked up, stepped closer so she could whisper real low. "Tishe."

"Devlin Tishe? Mystic Isle?"

A car turned onto St. Ann, almost crawling, the beams from the headlights bouncing off the walls of the building and off the two of them. Punch ducked under his arm and took off running. By the time he rounded the corner, she'd disappeared.

He looked for her for more than an hour, but never caught even a glimpse of her bright-red hair or skinny little body. Finally he climbed back in his car, drove down to Esplanade Avenue and parked beneath the sprawling branches of an oak tree.

All the lights were out at Mystic Isle. But he'd be back tomorrow when they were on. And he'd call Kathryn Morland, as well. He should have paid more attention to her complaints. He would now.

Her sister, Lisa, would probably be the next body washing up somewhere. Maybe even Kathryn herself. A man who'd killed once usually didn't hesitate to kill again.

Devlin Tishe. Mystic Isle. That was the last place he thought Raycine would have gone. She'd been so smart. But book smarts didn't always translate into street smarts or vice versa.

And Punch hadn't just been repeating idle rumors. She was far too scared for that. Devlin might not be the killer, but he was involved somehow. Or maybe he was the killer. Men in nice suits killed just like the ones from the projects. At least he was a place to start.

Ten minutes later, so tired he could barely hold his head up, Butch Ranklin drove back to his house and finally got a few decent hours' sleep.

LISA AWOKE to the melodic bell tones of her cell phone. The room was gray, just light enough that she could scamper across the floor to her phone without turning on her lamp. She hoped it wasn't Kathryn calling. She'd been glad for the opportunity to talk to her last night, but she didn't want to talk to her again, not until the time was right and there wouldn't have to be so many secrets between them.

"Hello?"

"Good morning, my sweet Lizemera."

Her heart jumped to her throat. "Devlin." She cradled the phone in her hands. "It's good to hear your voice."

"I have great news."

"You're coming out here to spend the day with me?"

"Better news than that."

"You're moving me back into town."

"Better even than that. I'm taking you away with me."

She fell back onto the bed and threw her legs into the air, fully awake, her spirits singing. "When?"

"For your birthday. I have it all planned, even have

our plane tickets. You and I will fly to Dallas and take care of the paperwork so that you can pick up your trust-fund check. Then we're flying to Paris for the trip of your life.''

"Paris, France?"

"What other Paris is there?"

She scooted off the bed and danced to the window to see the sun peek over the horizon. "I've always wanted to go to Paris. It sounds so totally romantic. Have you told Veretha yet?"

"No, but we had a major argument last night. She stormed out and didn't come home at all. I'm sure she understands that the marriage is virtually over. She knows I'm in love with you."

Paris, with her trust fund to live on and Devlin by her side. "You won't even have to work unless you want to. We can lie in bed and make love for hours on end."

"It sounds good, doesn't it, sweetheart?"

"Perfectly divine. I can't wait to tell my sister."

"No." His tone grew harsh. "You mustn't tell anyone. I don't want Veretha to know our plans until we've left the country. She'd manage to do something to spoil them."

"But I can't just fly to Paris without letting my sister know."

"Of course not. You can give her the news in person. Once we've taken care of the paperwork for your trust fund, we'll go to her office together and tell her that we're getting married as soon as my divorce is final. I've already talked to my lawyer. He can put it in process while we play on the French Riviera."

"Speaking of lawyers, I should call mine and let him know I'll be in to pick up my check that day."

"I've taken care of that, as well. I wanted to be certain my plan would work before I made our plane reservations."

"You think of everything, and now it's coming together just as you promised, Devlin. All the spirits must finally be lined up on our side."

"It's coming together perfectly," he agreed. "I have to go now. There are so many things I need to do to prepare for the trip and the changes in my life. Just remember, this is our secret."

"I will. I love you, Devlin."

Secrets. She had too many of them. She should have told Devlin what she and Roark were searching for. Why hadn't she? He knew Veretha was evil, that she couldn't be trusted. She was as evil as he was good.

She trusted Devlin. She did.

Still, she didn't call him back. Roark had said it was better to keep this between the two of them. But time was of the essence now if she expected to help Roark find information to prove Veretha had killed Raycine. That would certainly be grounds for divorce and get Veretha out of their lives for good.

She grabbed her warm robe and slipped her feet into her fuzzy slippers. Cottonmouth was a late sleeper. Mornings were a good time to work without having him burst in on her. She chanted a series of numbers in her head. Six, eight, four, two, seven. She'd found that series last night, typed in the middle of the investigation report Raycine had done before she left Tujacque's Manor.

The numbers made no sense and didn't seem to fit with anything else in the report. She had no idea what they meant, but she wanted to play with them a little, see if they led to anything.

She would have done it last night, but Cottonmouth had walked in on her and she'd closed the report, blanked the screen and yawned before announcing she'd had enough and was going to bed.

But the numbers had stayed in her mind.

VERETHA AWOKE to gentle stoking across her breasts. She rolled over, half asleep, half aroused, and fit herself into Devlin's arms.

"I missed you last night," he said. "Where did you go when you stormed away from the party?"

The dregs of sleep lifted as she remembered the events of the previous evening. Jealousy stirred inside her instantaneously, as if she'd touched a match to dry kindling. Just as quickly it switched to confusion. She'd been certain he'd wind up in Kathryn Richards's hotel room last night. But if he had, he'd have seen the snakes and known she'd delivered them to his newest playmate.

"I had a few drinks with some old friends," she said. "You seemed busy with a friend of your own. I didn't think you'd even notice I was gone."

"I don't know how many times I have to tell you that my dealings with other women are all business. They mean nothing to me."

"Not even Lisa Morland?"

"Lisa means a great deal—just a peg shy of twelve million bucks—but it's money you and I will enjoy together."

"I used to believe you when you said things like that. Thought it would be the way it was on our honeymoon. Do you remember our honeymoon, Devlin?"

"How could I forget?"

"We strolled down La Rambla as if we owned the

city and sipped wine in those quaint little sidewalk cafés.''

"And watched the flamenco dancers at Les Tarantes," he added, "then went back to our room where you danced for me and made love all night long.''

"Barcelona. Oh, Devlin, it was so wonderful. Why can't it be like that again?''

"There you go, spoiling my surprise.''

"What surprise?''

"Our second honeymoon. We're going to do it all again. Only this time, we won't have to worry about money.''

She swallowed her excitement. He'd made promises like this before when she'd gotten upset, anything to calm her down, but the promises had always melted like the ice in her tea on a hot summer day.

"You say these things, but they never happen.''

"This time they will. I have the plane reservations already, my sweet.''

She ignored her own thoughts of caution and let the excitement build inside her again, tiny trembles of anticipation. "When will we go?''

"December 8, late in the evening, with the money from Lisa's trust fund in hand.''

"How could you possibly have Lisa's money by then?''

"It's all taken care of. I'm flying with her to Dallas that morning. We're meeting with her attorney at ten. Then we'll go to the bank and she'll sign it over to me.''

"What makes you so sure she'll do that?''

"Because she thinks I'm leaving you, believes she and I will be flying to Paris. We'll leave all of this

behind, Veretha. New Orleans, Mystic Isle, the chance
of being arrested on murder charges.''

He pressed against her, so close she could feel the
hardness of him. She'd been wrong about him, about
so many things.

She was the one he loved, and they were going back
to Barcelona. In two short days.

ROARK HUNG UP the phone after talking to Lisa and
walked back toward the bedroom where Kathryn still
slept. He'd had her promise last night that she'd stay
away from Mystic Isle. Now he was going to ask her
to go back and find some way to keep Devlin busy for
the rest of the morning.

He hated the thought of her being anywhere near the
man, but this could be the breakthrough he'd be working for ever since he'd left northern Georgia and entered the world of Devlin Tishe. Apparently Lisa had
broken one password code and located a directory of
files that contained names of everyone who'd ever been
investigated by Devlin.

Margie's name had been there, along with an asterisk
and the letters *G M T,* followed by a three-digit number. She'd tried to figure out what the letters and numbers meant but got nowhere. He'd have to go out there
himself. The sooner the better.

Lisa could find a way to keep Cottonmouth busy. He
just had to make certain Devlin didn't pick today to go
calling on her. It was the most promising information
Lisa had come up with so far, but he knew better than
to let his hopes climb too high. The disappointment at
always finding he was merely running around in circles
was too deflating.

He knocked on the door of the bedroom, expecting

to find Kathryn still asleep. Instead, she was up, standing in front of the mirror, dressed in nothing but one of his skimpy white bath towels while she combed tangles from hair still wet from a shower.

The pent-up emotions of nine months exploded in a need so fierce he felt as if his legs might buckle under him. He couldn't possibly want a woman as much as he wanted Kathryn.

She turned and met his gaze. "What is it, Roark? Why are you looking at me like that?"

He searched his mind for a teasing offhand comment, a quip about her being dressed only in a smile and a towel. But he couldn't think at all. All he could do was feel a desire so consuming he couldn't possibly fight it off. He took a deep breath and exhaled it slowly. "I was just thinking how much I'd like to kiss you. I guess it would be a little out of line, though, under the circumstances."

The towel slipped an inch or two as she crossed the room and fit herself into his arms. And that was all the answer he needed.

Chapter Thirteen

Kathryn melted into Roark's kiss, threw herself into the thrill of it with an abandonment that would have amazed her if she'd stopped to think about it. But for once in her life, she didn't think or analyze or justify. She just kissed him again and again, long, deep, wet kisses that reached deep inside her, touched her soul.

She was aware when the towel slipped loose, felt it skim her hips and brush her thighs as it fell to her feet. She felt no embarrassment. The fact that her body was bare seemed far less significant than the fact that she was exposing her vulnerabilities and still wasn't afraid. Didn't feel that she could have pulled away even if she'd wanted to. All she felt was a rightness, and a certainty that they'd been moving toward this since the moment they'd met.

Roark's hand skimmed her rib cage, his thumbs riding the swell of her breasts, then massaging her nipples until they were pebbled and erect, as if begging to be sucked and fondled and caressed. He kissed her mouth, the hollow of her neck, the tip of each breast. And with each touch, the fire inside her grew hotter.

They moved as one across the room and dropped to the bed. She tucked shaking fingers beneath the fabric

of his shirt and struggled to unbutton it. By the time
she'd finished, he'd unbuckled his belt and unsnapped
his black jeans. She stretched across the bed and
watched him strip naked, trembled at the sight of him,
knew he was the most beautiful man she'd ever seen.
Lean, but muscular, bronzed skin, white only at the
area his running shorts covered. Sparse dark hairs dot-
ted his abdomen. And below that, he was hard and
aroused and...

And she'd never wanted a man more.

He stretched out beside her, raised himself on one
elbow and looked into her eyes as he stroked her
breasts and belly with his free hand. She trembled, so
aware of every touch of his fingers that she was already
moist and aching for him. Yet she read more than desire in his eyes, sensed a hesitancy that made her heart
almost stop beating. This was so right for her. How
could it be wrong for him?

She touched the curve of his lips with her fingertips,
wishing he would just kiss her and not look at her the
way he was right now.

Instead, he took her hand in his. "I didn't plan this,
Kathryn. I don't—I mean, I hope you know this isn't
connected to Mystic Isle. This is just about us."

It had never occurred to her that it could be anything
else until he'd brought it up. Now the doubts filled her
mind. "What made you say that, Roark?"

"Working with Devlin Tishe for the last nine
months. Witnessing a constant overdose of sex and sen-
suality used as tools of the trade."

The warmth that had filled her a few seconds ago
turned cold. "Have there been so many?"

"For Devlin?"

"For you, Roark. Have you had so many?"

"Women? For me?" He stared as if her question was too incredible to comprehend.

"Isn't that what you meant?"

He kissed her again, softly, as if she would break. "There haven't been so many, Kathryn. There haven't been *any,* not since I came to New Orleans. I've been too involved in the investigation. I thought that would be obvious."

"Nothing about you is obvious, Roark Lansing. You're the most mysterious and exciting man I've ever been with."

"That's the fake Roark Lansing, Kathryn. The real me is just an ordinary guy. Strip me of the black clothes and clouds of illusion and this is what you get."

"Make love with me, Roark, whoever you are. Just make love with me. I need this moment in time. I need it with you."

And he did.

He fit himself inside her, thrusting deeper and deeper, driving her to the very edge of delirium before erupting with her in a climax so intense she thought her heart might burst from her chest.

She lay beside him, their bodies slick and warm, his words still playing in her mind. He thought he was two men. She saw him as one. Sexy and strong, seductive and protective.

She'd have liked to lie there forever, bathed in the afterglow until their strength returned, and then make love again and again. But the real world was waiting outside their door. Still, it was Roark who made the first move, kissed her again, then slipped from her arms.

"I have some business to take care of," he said.

"Then I'll take you to the hotel to check out and pick up your things."

"No thanks. I'll just go buy new things. I don't think I ever want to touch anything in that room again. I'll expect snakes to crawl out of the pockets and from between the layers of loose fabric."

"Then go shopping." He pulled on his black jeans and snapped them at the waist. "But stay away from Mystic Isle."

"But—"

"No buts. We made a bargain."

She shrugged.

"I'm serious, Kathryn."

"How can you think just going to Mystic Isle is dangerous for me and yet you won't tell me where Lisa is so that I can go and insist she come back to Dallas with me? It doesn't add up, Roark."

"You trusted me a little while ago, Kathryn. You couldn't have made love the way we did if you hadn't. You have to keep trusting me and you have to trust Lisa, as well."

"That's not so easy, not when you tell me so little. What is it Lisa's doing that's so important?"

He walked back to the bed and took both her hands in his. "If I told you more, you'd worry more, and I'm doing enough of that for both of us. But I promise that if I ever think that Lisa is in immediate danger, I'll get her out of there."

"But what if you make a mistake, Roark? What if you don't see it coming in time to stop it?"

He stared at her, saying nothing. But his silence said it all. He couldn't guarantee a thing. Finally he turned away and pulled on his shirt.

"Go shopping, Kathryn. Go to the zoo. Ride the

streetcar to Camellia Grill for breakfast. Do something to occupy your mind, but stay away from Devlin, Veretha and Mystic Isle. That's all I ask. That was the bargain we made. And if you need to talk to me—about anything at all—call my cell phone.''

It was a damn poor bargain when Lisa's life was at stake.

ROARK RUSHED OUT of the house and climbed behind the wheel of his car. He'd been a fool even to consider sending Kathryn back to Mystic Isle. Fortunately he'd realized that in time. He was starting to realize a lot of other things, as well, mainly that what he'd been thinking of as attraction and concern for her went a lot deeper than that.

Inconceivable that feelings that had lain dormant since his wife had died years ago would surface now, when every core of his being should be focused on what he had to do. Then again, maybe that was what it had taken to make him let down his guard and put his feelings on the line again.

When this was over, he'd have to deal with whatever was going on between him and Kathryn. Face the fact that the heart he thought was numb might have sprung back to life.

Right now, he had to deal with the problems flying in his face. It was only a matter of time until someone connected Raycine to Mystic Isle, and when they did the police would come calling. Devlin would run. Nine months ago Roark would have killed him in cold blood before he'd let him get off scot-free. A week ago, he might have done the same.

But Raycine had most likely died because of something she'd found out, information she'd been trying to get to him. Getting the evidence to put Devlin away for good was still important, but not as important as making sure Lisa and Kathryn Morland stayed alive.

He'd go to Tujacque's Manor this morning, check out the latest clue that Lisa had found and try one last time to come up with irrevocable proof that Devlin had a hand in the deaths of at least two young women—maybe more. But if he came away empty-handed this time, he was going to insist that Lisa stop investigating. The risk was too great, the danger too imminent.

Lisa's birthday was in two days. The prospect of getting his hands on all that money before he cut out would have Devlin's instincts razor-sharp. Veretha understood that, too, was worried that Devlin was leaving without her. That was the only explanation for her going out of control last night and dumping those snakes in Kathryn's hotel room.

The heat was on. For all of them.

RANKLIN SAT at a booth in the back of his favorite neighborhood dive and dialed the cell-phone number Kathryn Morland had supplied. He pictured her in his mind as the phone rang, sitting in that chair in his office, trying to convince him that Devlin Tishe had something to do with her sister's disappearance. He didn't usually take missing-person reports, but she'd insisted on seeing someone with rank, and he'd been the only guy available. Strange how things worked out.

Raycine had been dead even then. Strangled, thrown into a vehicle and driven to St. John's Bayou to be dumped into a watery grave. That was pretty well all the information they'd been able to determine at this point. If it turned out Devlin Tishe was behind Raycine's murder, he'd owe a lot to a waif who lived on the streets.

The phone stopped in the middle of a ring.

"Kathryn."

"Good morning, Miss Morland. This is Detective Ranklin. I took the report on your sister last week."

"I remember. Do you have some news?"

"No news, but I'd like to ask you a few more questions."

"Of course."

"You may have heard about my daughter's body being found this week." God, it hurt to say that out loud. He thought about it all the time, but it still almost killed him to have to say it.

"I heard. I'm sorry."

"Thanks. The reason I'm calling is I think Raycine was also involved in the work of Devlin Tishe, that she may have been one of his followers. I think that may be what got her killed."

"Why would he kill her?"

"Raycine was very smart, close to genius range, a whiz at everything technical. I think she may have found out something Devlin didn't want her to know. A secret he'd commit murder to keep from being exposed."

KATHRYN WAS SHAKING by the time she finished the short conversation with Detective Ranklin. If Raycine was connected to Mystic Isle, Roark would know it. He'd had plenty of opportunity to say something to her about that, yet he'd chosen not to.

Maybe it wasn't Devlin and Veretha who were dangerous. Maybe it was Roark. He said he was two men. One mysterious, who wasn't at all what he seemed, one who'd admitted lying to her about so many things. The other, just an ordinary man. But there was nothing ordinary about Roark Lansing.

She grabbed the black dress she'd worn last night and slipped into it, then shoved her feet into the black pumps. All bets were off, all promises null and void. She was going to do what she'd come here to do.

Mystic Isle was only a short cab ride away.

KATHRYN SAT in a comfortable, upholstered chair in Devlin's office, smiling as he gave her the once-over, letting his gaze linger longer than necessary on the green sweater she'd bought on the way over. The fit was intentionally snug as was the fit of the darker green slacks. She smiled and leaned forward.

"I guess I should have called first."

"Not at all. I was hoping you'd come in."

"I just wanted to tell you what a great time I had last night."

"So did I," Devlin answered, "at least while we were together in the garden. I was afraid I'd done something to upset you when you were ready to rush off so fast after that."

"It was just a headache. I get them occasionally. When I do, the only way I can get rid of them is to get a good night's sleep."

"Which you must have done. You look radiant this morning."

"I do feel much better, but I've been thinking about what you said last night about communicating with my great-grandmother. I'd really like to try and contact her."

"I believe you're making the right decision. When a person feels the need as strongly as you do, it's usually for a reason. As I told you last night, it's a complex process and not always successful.''

"I understand that. I'm willing to take that risk and to pay you whatever it costs.''

"The fee is negotiable. Right now I think we should just concentrate on the first step in the process. We need to spend time together.'' He got up from his chair, walked over and shut the office door, turning the lock as he did. "Come sit by me on the sofa so that we can connect more intimately, like old friends. I need to know everything about you, so that when the spirits are present they sense the total unity between us.''

She swallowed and tried to hide the revulsion seething inside her. "I know the bonding process is important, but my time is very limited. I'd like to try to go straight to the communication process itself. Besides, I already feel a bond with you, Devlin, as if I knew you long before we met.''

At least she knew about him. She wasn't certain how going through the channeling session would help her, except that she needed to experience what Lisa must have experienced. Needed to see what kind of techniques Devlin used and see if he called on the spirits to convince people to go to some special place. What she needed was some clue about Lisa's whereabouts. If she could see her in person, she would at least know for certain her sister was safe and not being held prisoner until Devlin found a way to get his hands on her trust fund.

A location was all she needed. Detective Ranklin would do the rest.

"It's risky to go to the spirits unprepared. If you make them angry, they may not ever help you cross the barriers that separate the living from the dead.''

"Still, I'd like to try. I have a check already written for ten thousand dollars. I'm willing to pay more if you ask."

"Very well, Kathryn. I don't feel good about this, but I'm willing to go along with your request."

Amazing how money talked, even in the spirit world. "When can we start?"

"We must prepare ourselves. I'll take you to the Serenity Room, where you can sit and meditate and try to cleanse your mind of every worldly thought. While you do that, I'll meditate, as well. As I said, going to the spirits to plead on your behalf consumes much of my strength and requires my full concentration. When the time is right, I'll come for you."

More likely he'd come when the equipment was set up, but she had to admit that Devlin was convincing. It was difficult to listen to him talk without getting the sense that you were about to enter another dimension, a place where life and death merged and spirits moved freely between the two. It gave even a cynic like herself the creeps.

"Come with me, Kathryn. The spirits await."

COTTONMOUTH KNEW that Veretha and Devlin would want to know about the stuff Lisa was looking at on the computer this morning. When he'd told Veretha, she'd thanked him for calling, promised she'd bring him a surprise the next time she came out. He hoped it was one of those books with naked babes in it. The ones he had were so old the corners of the pages had started tearing. He liked looking at beautiful women. That was why he liked having Lisa around.

Margie had been beautiful like Lisa, only her hair had been dark and she'd had a laugh that made you think of sunshine. Her eyes had seemed to dance when she looked at you, and her skin was so soft it had made him think of the sugary cotton candy his parents bought him at the state fair when he was a kid. Just touch your lips to it and it melted into pure sugar. Margie was really special, but she'd made a mistake. Devlin didn't tolerate mistakes.

Cottonmouth ducked out of the morning sunshine and through the door of the old shed behind Tujacque's Manor. It was dark and moldy inside, filled with garden tools no one ever used. Not much of a hangout, but he came here often. The spot provided a perfect view into Lisa's room, especially at night when her lights were on. He'd stand out here all alone, watching, hoping to catch a glimpse of her dancing around the room in her bra and panties or in one of those short flouncy gowns she wore.

Some nights he got all excited just watching her. Long legs, nice perky breasts, shiny blond hair. He'd watch and he'd think about the times Devlin was up there with her, inside her room with the door locked. Devlin always said they were talking business, but Cottonmouth knew better. He'd sneak up the stairs and stand outside the door, listening to the squeals and moans and the squeaking of the worn bedsprings.

But you couldn't blame Devlin. He was trying to appease the good and evil spirits, and some days he had to give in to the evil ones. Cottonmouth understood, but still he shouldn't cheat on Veretha. That was why Cottonmouth called her and told her every time Devlin showed up at the old plantation house.

While he was staring at the house, Lisa opened the back door and stepped out. There was a chill to the air, but she didn't seem to notice. He was all bundled up in his old army fatigue jacket, but all she had on was a pair of tight jeans and a sweater that showed every curve.

A need rumbled inside him—the evil spirits talking to him, reminding him what it had been like before Devlin had taught him a better way. It wasn't right to lust. Devlin had taught him that. It wasn't right to kill, either, unless you had a very good reason or the spirits made you do it, sort of the way they made Devlin come out here and get it on with Lisa even though he had a beautiful wife at home.

Lisa was fine, though. He liked her. Still, she'd made a mistake and started snooping around. And the Tishes just didn't tolerate mistakes.

ROARK STARED at the name on the computer screen— Margie Slaton. *His* Margie. The fact that her name even appeared on a list stored on Devlin's hard drive bit into him like a nail hammered through his heart. But all it proved was that she'd had some connection to the workings of Mystic Isle. And he'd already known that.

"The letters and numbers after the names must mean something," Lisa said, "but I can't figure out what."

"They could refer to a file where more information is stored, maybe a password-protected file on the hard drive or a file on one of the floppy disks or a CD."

"I searched and couldn't find a thing."

"Everything is likely in code." He scrolled down the list of names, checking the codes. "There appear to be about a dozen different letter/number combinations. That would suggest a dozen files." He did a couple of quick file searches and came up with nothing.

"The disks are all labeled with names," she said. "I checked them all while I was waiting for you. None of them were identified with a series of letters and numbers.''

''Which means we'll have to go through and check each disk individually. And we need to work fast. If Cottonmouth starts nosing around, one of us will have to go keep him busy with some fake emergency.''

''I can find some reason to get him outside,'' Lisa said. ''He loves talking to me.''

He inserted a new disk, this one labeled Awakenings. He typed in some commands and began checking all the data stored on the disk, hoping to find something that would match the series of letters and numbers that had followed Margie's name. There was nothing on the disk except equipment descriptions, the date each item was purchased and the purchase price. He yanked it out and inserted another.

''This could take forever, Roark. We don't have forever. I won't be here much longer.''

''Good. I was going to suggest that if we don't find what we're looking for this morning, you should get out of here.''

''I'm not running away. I'm not afraid anymore— not even of Veretha.''

''What changed your mind?''

''Devlin.'' There was a ring to her voice. Light. Excited.

''What did Devlin say?''

''I can't tell you yet, but you'll know soon. Everyone will know. Even Kathryn. The spirits are smiling on us.''

Spirits—good, evil or indifferent. How could they always be on the side of Devlin Tishe?

DEVLIN LED KATHRYN through the door of the Awakening Room. It was cold and damp, as if a light mist were falling. "I want you to lie down on the sofa and relax," he said. "Try not be afraid. If the spirits sense fear and mistrust, they won't appear or talk to us."

She stretched out on the white sofa, but she didn't relax. Devlin turned a switch on the wall and the lighting dimmed until everything was bathed in a golden glow. A haunting melody played in the background and the scent of honeysuckle filled the room. Her head grew light, as if she was floating. A chill went through her, and she had the crazy feeling that someone or something had just entered the room.

"Take a deep breath, Kathryn, and be prepared. The first spirit is already with us."

Chapter Fourteen

Kathryn felt dizzy, as if the room were spinning. She closed her eyes, and when she opened them again, the motion seemed to have slowed to a gentle rocking.

Devlin leaned over and put his mouth to her ear. "You are in luck. The air is rich with the promise of many spirits. The other world has been trying to reach you."

"Kathryn. Kathryn, can you hear me?"

The voice was low, female and sounded as if it were coming through a tunnel, traveling from a long way off. The notion was so eerie and spine-tingling Kathryn had to remind herself where she was and that the sensations and voices came from the sophisticated equipment she'd viewed behind the curtain the night Roark had found her snooping around this part of the house.

Roark. Even then, she'd reeled from an attraction so strong that his slightest touch had affected her and one look into his dark eyes had sent tingles up her spine.

"You are drifting away from us, Kathryn. The spirits will leave if you're not ready."

"I'm here." And since she was, she needed to go into the pseudo spiritual encounter with as much fervor as she could muster, and appear to do so as naively as no doubt Lisa had. Let Devlin lead. She only had to follow.

"Hold on to me," he whispered as he scooted his chair closer and took her left hand in his. "If you become too afraid or feel yourself slipping into the other world, just squeeze my hand really hard. I'll hold you and keep you grounded in this one."

"Please don't lose me to the spirits, Devlin." The words practically gagged her, but they should convince him that she was as gullible as the next sucker.

"I won't let anything happen to you, Kathryn. I'm here for you. Are you afraid?"

"A little." She wasn't totally sure that wasn't the truth.

"Don't be afraid, but be prepared. You may feel you are being pulled first one way and then another, and you'll experience sensations that seem out of place in this space." He turned away and scanned the room, slowly, as if searching for something. "The spirits are gathering now, and the tension is building. I sense anxiety and friction among those who would join us."

A noise swept through the room, a gentle wave of sound like a breeze tickling the leaves of the elm that grew outside her house back in Dallas. It was reassuring at first, but as it intensified and grew louder, her insides began to roll.

"Kathryn."

This time the voice was crystal-clear, though she couldn't tell where it was coming from. It seemed to move about the room, floating somewhere above her, as if it had materialized from thin air. She looked up. A wispy white cloud fluttered like a butterfly, circling the room just beneath the ceiling.

"Kathryn, I miss you. Come over and visit me."

This time the voice had a ghostly quality that set the hairs on the back of her neck on end.

"I'm not sure who's talking to you, Kathryn," Devlin said, "but feel free to answer."

Kathryn grew uneasy at the idea of speaking to floating voices, but she was here to find out exactly how Devlin worked and to experience what others did while in this room.

"Kathryn, do you need me?" This time the voice was male.

She took a deep breath and exhaled slowly before responding. "Who are you?"

"One who loves you. Come join us, my dear."

"I can't come. You must talk to me here."

"Then tell us what you want us to help you with."

"Why do you think I need help?"

"Your heart is troubled. I sense your fears."

"Do you see danger?"

"I see you all alone. You need someone to hold you. To hold you. Hold you. Hold you…" The voice dissolved and faded, echoing as if it were two or even three voices.

Her blood ran cold. She hadn't expected it to seem this real.

"Kathryn, you must fight fear," a voice said now.

"How can I do that?"

"Peace. Harmony. Love." The words seemed to bounce off the walls and fill the room, the volume going up and down on each syllable.

"Be careful who you trust, Kathryn. Be careful. Very careful."

"How will I know who to trust?"

"Trust your heart. Always trust your heart." All the voices spoke in unison, then quieted. The room grew icy cold, but she felt as if a warm gloved hand moved across her body, starting at her head and traveling all the way to her feet.

The music changed to a beating rhythm, and her pulse increased, building until her heartbeat was in sync. The room was filled with clouds now, but they were a grayish blue and tumultuous, rolling across the ceiling and coming so low they grazed her skin.

"Seek the truth, Kathryn."

"Who's speaking to me?"

"A spirit who wanders the world of the dead. I lost the truth. Don't let that happen to you."

"How will I know who speaks the truth?"

"He will knock on your heart's door. Let him in. Let him in, Kathryn. Don't wander away from the truth."

"I'm here with you, Kathryn." This time the voice was Devlin's, reassuring, comforting. "I can't control the spirits today. They are fearful for you and they are demanding that I let them speak."

"Kathryyyyyn."

She shuddered. The cold had moved into her bones, was penetrating the deepest recesses of her soul. She was trying hard to hold on to reality, but she felt it slipping away. The spirits were here with her.

No. There were no spirits. It was a ruse. She couldn't let go of that fact or she'd drown in the same fate that had claimed Lisa.

"Kathryyyyyyn." This time the voice was sharp and crackly, like a very old woman—or a witch.

"Who's calling me?"

"Don't you know?"

"No. I don't know."

"You forget so easily. Be very careful, Kathryn. Be

very, very careful. Be very careful of..." The voice faded to silence.

"Please don't go away without finishing what you were going to say." Her chest seemed to be constricting, tightening around her heart. She flailed her arms about wildly, trying to reach out to the spirit, but she touched nothing but air. Voices started flying at her from everywhere.

"Leave that baby alone."

"You can't escape."

"Devlin can help her."

"It's too cold here. I want to go back."

"Please let me near her. I'm the one she needs."

Panic swelled inside Kathryn. "Stop. Please, just stop. I don't understand what you're trying to tell me."

"Do you want me to ask them to go away, Kathryn?" Devlin's voice washed over her like a silk blanket, soothing and exotic all at once.

"No. Not yet."

"Then sit up and slide into my arms so that I can hold you and keep you safe."

She did, just as a sea of water rose in front of her, splashing, crashing against an invisible wall. She held on to Devlin as an unseen force tried to pull her into the swirling dark waters. It wasn't touching her, yet it was sucking her breath away.

But Devlin was holding her, caressing her, keeping her safe. "You want to be safe and loved, Kathryn. That's all they're trying to tell you. You must face that truth, give yourself a chance to find happiness, give in to love."

All of a sudden there was a loud clamoring of voices, angry, bellowing voices that screeched and squawked and broke the semi-trance she'd drifted into.

Devlin let go of her and jumped from his chair. "Stay here, Kathryn. Don't move from the couch." He rushed to the curtain and slipped through it, leaving her with the horrible screeching noises. Ignoring Devlin's command, she crossed the room and peeked around the curtain just in time to see Veretha peering around the corner of a back door that had been left open. Devlin's concentration on the piece of equipment he was examining was so intense he didn't realize she was standing there and probably hadn't seen Veretha, either.

Kathryn eased the curtain back into place and walked out of the room and toward the steps. She'd seen and heard enough. The images and illusions had been so effective that they had drawn her into the chimera, had her heart pounding and her mind defying logic and reason.

The only thing the encounter had taught her was that Devlin was a dangerously deceptive man surrounded by dangerous people. She still had no idea where to find Lisa.

She raced down the steps, not slowing until she reached the exit, stepped outside and breathed in a heaping gulp of fresh air. Everything she did led her deeper into a pit of phantasm and illusion, the creepy frightening world of Devlin Tishe, but nothing led her to Lisa. There was no one to help her separate myth from fact. No one to trust.

She started walking as fast as she could, heading toward the street. A hand wrapped around her arm and jerked her to a stop. "Do promises mean nothing to you?"

She stared at Roark. His tone was rough, and his hand clutched her arm so tightly it hurt. But if he thought she could be intimidated by him, he was sadly mistaken. "Does lying mean nothing to you, Roark Lansing?"

"What are you talking about?"

"I'm talking about Raycine Ranklin and why you never mentioned that she was one of Devlin's followers."

"I didn't think it was important."

"Surely you can come up with a better excuse than that."

"Okay, I didn't want to worry you."

"No, you think I should just go back to Dallas. Tend to my own business. Don't make waves. And while I'm at it, why don't I just pretend Lisa is at Girl Scout Camp?"

"I didn't say that."

"You don't have a say at all, not since you won't tell me where she is or why I can't see her."

"Keep your voice down."

"I've kept my voice low, kept my temper and kept my sanity, but I'm just about to lose all of those things."

"How did you find out about Raycine?"

"Her father told me. Seems he finally realizes that I wasn't delusional when I suggested that Lisa's involvement with Mystic Isle had led to her disappearance. Apparently his daughter disappeared for a while before she was murdered. Just dropped out of sight and lost touch with all her friends. He's on to all of you, so maybe you're the one who should be worried."

"When did you talk to Ranklin?"

"This morning after you left."

"That explains your sudden change in attitude."

"Level with me, Roark. For once, just tell me the

straight truth. Is Lisa in the same place Raycine was before she was murdered?''

He hesitated. ''Can't we talk about this somewhere else?''

''We don't need to talk. You just answered my question.''

''I'm on your side, Kathryn. I think Lisa should return to Dallas with you. But she's a grown woman and she makes her own decisions.''

''I doubt that. I think Devlin is making the decisions for all of you. You're just puppets who dance when he pulls the strings.''

''I'm not dangling from anyone's strings, but I don't suppose anything I say will convince you of that.''

''You can take me to Lisa.''

''That's not an option right now.''

''Then stay out of my way, because I'm not going to stand by and watch Devlin call the shots. I will not just sit around and wait for Lisa's body to be hauled out of some damn murky bayou.''

He exhaled sharply. ''No, you want to see if you can't get killed yourself. That would really help. Go back to Dallas, Kathryn. Trust me, that's the best thing you can do right now.''

''Go back to Dallas. Why? Because you say I should? Well, that reason doesn't cut it with me. You've already admitted that you've lied to me ever since we met. I don't know one good reason to listen to you now, and I certainly don't trust you.''

He glanced back toward Mystic Isle. She followed his gaze. Devlin was standing in the doorway staring at them.

''I can't stand out here and argue about this, Kathryn. Go back to my apartment and wait for me. I'll be there as soon as I can get free.''

''I'd sooner go back to my room full of snakes.'' She turned and stormed down the walk. She was scared for Lisa and angry at herself for falling so hard and fast for a man who thought that truth was whatever he decided it was at the time. And she was furious with Detective Ranklin for waiting until his own daughter's body was discovered before he was willing to deal with Devlin Tishe.

If you don't get Lisa away from there, she'll be dead before her birthday.

The words of the caller echoed in her mind, growing louder and louder as she walked aimlessly down Esplanade Avenue. Was it Raycine who had called that night to warn her? Had that been her last act before she was killed?

Get Lisa out. But get her out of where?

And why did it hurt so much to know that she'd made a mistake in believing Roark was any different from everyone else she'd met since arriving in New Orleans? Like the rest of them, he had his own agenda, and helping her wasn't on it.

VERETHA RAN her thumb down the page of the phone book, stopping at the number of the only airline she hadn't called yet, her temper getting closer to the exploding point with every connection. None of them had a reservation for Devlin and her to Barcelona. None had a reservation for her to anywhere. The only reservations she'd been able to confirm had been two seats on Continental Airlines for Devlin Tishe and Lisa Morland to fly to Dallas.

She dialed the number, then drummed her fingers on

the desk while she was stuck on hold to wait for the next available representative. As the minutes ticked by, she let her mind go over the years she'd spent with Devlin. He'd always had an eye for the women, but he'd loved her in the beginning. She was almost certain of that. But they'd grown apart over the past year. It had all started with Margie Slaton.

"Sorry to keep you waiting. How may I help you?"

Finally. "I'd like to confirm the reservations for my husband and me to Barcelona, Spain, for the evening of December 8."

"Could you spell the last name for me?"

She spelled the name, then gave their first names. The wait seemed interminable, though she didn't expect the woman to find any such reservations. Devlin had no intention of taking her anywhere. She'd suspected it from the second she'd realized he was in the Awakening Room with his new girlfriend. That was why she'd sabotaged the routine, turned on all the speakers at once.

"We don't have a flight to Barcelona scheduled for December 8. Wait, I have a flight to the Cayman Islands for—no, I'm sorry that's a different first name and only for one. Could the flight be on another day or another airline?"

"You're right. I just looked at it wrong. I'm sorry to have bothered you."

And that was that. Devlin was no doubt leaving, but his traveling companion would be Lisa Morland's trust fund. He could pick up lots of women with twelve million dollars. He'd be living the good life. She'd be left to face the music.

Only it wasn't going to work that way. She'd make

certain of that. It wouldn't be all that difficult. Dead women didn't get trust funds.

Tonight would be the grand finale, her last time to reign as priestess, her last night with Devlin, her last night in New Orleans. The plan was already forming in her mind. Her last night should be one to remember. She was nothing if not dramatic.

ROARK KNEW the apartment was empty the minute he opened the door. The feeling was different, colder, lonelier than it had been when he'd left this morning. He never should have made love with Kathryn, but he was glad that he had. It had been the only humanizing thing he'd done in the past nine months. He'd reached out and touched someone intimately, someone honest and brave, someone risking all for someone other than herself. Someone who had made him realize he was capable of caring again.

He didn't blame her for being angry with him, but that didn't change the fact that he couldn't tell her where Lisa was. It would be like signing her death certificate. The second she went storming out to Tujacque's Manor, Devlin would know, and he would never let Kathryn stand between him and Lisa's trust fund.

The money was all but in his hands, though it wasn't there yet, and he was running scared. Roark had seen the fear in his eyes and read the apprehension in his movements after Detective Butch Ranklin's unofficial visit to Mystic Isle this afternoon. Veretha was feeling the strain, too. She'd been nervous, so antsy she could barely stand still when she'd come into the shop to remind Roark about tonight.

Mystic Isle and everything connected to it was about

to go up in smoke. Devlin would probably walk away unscathed. Nine months of work, of planning and scheming and living a life he hated, and Roark had accomplished nothing. Worse, he'd let Raycine die as needlessly as Margie had.

Tomorrow morning he'd go to Detective Ranklin and give him the information he'd gathered—evidence of a sophisticated scam operation, suspicion in the deaths of two young women. Probably too little too late, but he'd also tell them about Tujacque's Manor, and hopefully Ranklin could go out and talk some sense into Lisa Morland. Who knew what Devlin had planned for her once the money was in his hands?

And once it was all over Kathryn would go back to her life. He'd go back to his. It would have probably never worked between them anyway. They didn't really know each other. Their only link had been their mistrust of Devlin. He'd wanted revenge. Kathryn had only wanted to rescue her sister.

What he'd felt for her was an attraction and a bond born of desperation. If they'd met in any other situation, they probably wouldn't have even noticed each other.

Yeah, right. And if he was walking over hot coals, he probably wouldn't notice a pool of cold water right in front of his nose.

KATHRYN STOOD in the security-check line at the airport. She was traveling light, carrying only her handbag, the dress she'd worn to the party last night and a couple of magazines she'd picked up in the airport gift shop. The Ponchartrain Hotel was shipping her the things she'd left in her room, guaranteed snake-free. Detective Ranklin had taken care of that.

She'd met with him again late this afternoon, told him everything she'd discovered about Devlin and Veretha Tishe, Roark Lansing and Mystic Isle. The attorney handling Lisa's trust fund had called while Ranklin was with her. He'd just gotten back to his office to find a message saying Lisa would be in before noon tomorrow to pick up her check.

Ranklin was certain Lisa wouldn't be arriving alone. He'd assured her that someone from the Dallas Police Department would be on hand to make certain Lisa was not doing anything against her will and to arrest Devlin, if he was with her, on charges of running a scam operation.

Kathryn would be there, as well. Everything was under control. There was no reason for the fear that ground in her stomach, no reason for her blood to run so cold. No reason for the dread still eating away at her like a caterpillar devouring a leaf.

The warning ran through her mind again. *Dead before her birthday.* The voice was inside her head, not an apparition like the ones Devlin had produced in the Awakening Room, but just as clear and twice as frightening. She staggered backward at the sudden onslaught of emotion.

Something was dreadfully wrong. She didn't know how she knew it, but she was as certain of that as she'd ever been of anything.

Her cell phone shrilled. Her fingers were shaking as she punched the talk button. *Please let it be Lisa.*

"Kathryn."

"Hi, it's me, Punch. I've got some news for you."

Kathryn's pulse rate skyrocketed. "Do you know where my sister is?"

"Kind of."

"Where?"

"She's in some plantation house outside of town. Belongs to some rich woman who lets Devlin Tishe use it."

"Where is this house?"

"I don't know."

The hope that had swelled a second ago deflated. "Do you know the name of the woman who owns the plantation?"

"No, but I do know where Veretha Tishe is going to be tonight. If you go there, you might find someone who knows about the plantation."

"Where?"

"It's over in Algiers, not close to the ferry, though. It's down in the lower part, out in the woods, down where nobody lives and nobody much goes."

"Why will she be there?"

"That's where she holds her meetings."

"What kind of meetings?"

"Look, I gotta give the phone back to this guy who let me use it. I'll tell you how to find the place, then I gotta go."

"Will you be at the meeting?"

"Me? No way. I'm scared of that voodoo stuff. If Veretha puts a curse on you, there ain't no breaking it. You're just cursed, that's all. Now you wanna know where it's at or not?"

Kathryn stepped out of the security-check line and wrote down the directions. She'd have to rent a car and she still might not be able to find the place. It was probably a stupid move, especially as Ranklin said everything was under control.

But the feeling that Lisa was in danger persisted. "Thanks, Punch," she said.

Kathryn hurried back to the baggage area and the car-rental counters. She had an almost uncontrollable urge to call Roark and tell him where she was going. She squelched it. Nothing had changed. There was no reason to trust him.

Besides, this was just a meeting. Voodoo or not, there would be lots of people there. What could possibly go wrong?

Chapter Fifteen

Clouds hovered low, cutting off the light of the moon and stars. The road was dark, deserted, with few signs to guide the way. Without the landmarks Punch had provided, Kathryn would never have found the winding back road that led to the meeting spot. Even the landmarks were difficult to make out in the beams of her headlights—a towering cypress tree split by lightning, a barn that had lost its roof in a hurricane, a lonely, old steeple that had survived the church it used to top by a century or more.

By the time she made the last turn, she'd begun to fear that Punch had sent her to a place that didn't exist. There had been no sign of life for a good half hour. She was just about to give up, turn around and try to find her way back to civilization when she saw a fiery glow rising like a noxious gas over the swampy land in front of her.

As she drove closer, she found the source of the illumination. Torches had been staked into the ground, interspersed with gas lanterns, all of them placed in a circular pattern. There was a square wooden platform in the center of the circle that seemed to be the focal

point for a group of about forty people who crowded
around it.

She slowed and parked at the back of a line of cars
and pickup trucks that had stopped at the end of a dead-
end road. It was not the best of spots. As she stepped
out of the car, her foot sank into a bog that practically
sucked the shoe from her foot. She chose her ground
carefully after that, looking for higher, drier spots to
plant her feet, though not always finding them.

No one seemed to notice her approach or care. The
people were absorbed in activities taking place on the
platform. All of a sudden the crowd broke into a chant.
The words appeared to be a hodgepodge of English,
African and Cajun. The only parts of the chant she
understood were the words *curse, devil, death, sacrifice,* but that was enough to turn her skin to gooseflesh.

She pushed her way through the crowd, determined
to see what was going on. The crowd began to sway
and swing their arms over their heads, their voices
growing louder. She was being shoved about, propelled
to the front. And then the chant changed to one word:
Veretha. Veretha. Veretha.

And there she was, front and center, her long black
hair swinging wildly as she danced across the platform,
moving so gracefully her bare feet barely touched the
floor. She was stunning, dressed in nothing but silky
white veils that hugged her breasts and swaying hips
and swished about the dangling silver jewelry at her
ankles.

Kathryn inched closer, squeezed through a cluster of
women who had started a dance of their own. Veretha
shouted a new chant, something about casting a gris-
gris on someone's evil-eyed man. One of the women
ran to the edge of the platform and bowed in front of

Veretha, evidently the woman whose man had the evil eye.

Veretha jumped from the platform and danced around the woman, then reached down and lifted the lid from a round wicker basket. A rattlesnake stuck out its head and began to crawl from the wicker container. Vertha grabbed him in one smooth swoop.

The crowd cheered, but jumped backward, giving Veretha and the snake more room. She twirled and danced, sticking her face in the face of the snake, so close it would seem the snake would surely bury its fangs in her lips. But the snake merely wrapped itself around her arm.

When the crowd was worked to a fever pitch, she lifted the lid to the basket again. This time a green snake crawled out. She picked it up and threw it around her neck like a lei. The snake tangled in her hair and curled about her arm. Kathryn stared at the snakes, seeing them, but thinking of the dozens that had crawled around her hotel room last night. The memories and the sights combined to mesmerize her. She stood still as Veretha twirled wildly, the snakes curling around her arms and body, their tongues flicking in and out of their mouths.

Suddenly the chants stopped and the crowd grew quiet. Veretha no longer danced. She was standing at the edge of the platform, staring into the crowd. It took only a few seconds for Kathryn to realize that all eyes were on her. She met Veretha's cold stare and in that split second knew what was going to happen next.

Veretha held the neck of the rattlesnake and began to twirl the reptile over her head like a rope. Kathryn tried to run, but the people surged around her, blocking her path. The snake left Veretha's hand to hurtle through the air, heading directly for her. The tail end of it slapped her face, and she began to shove and push her way through the crowd, not caring who she hit with her flailing arms.

She ran blindly, her feet sinking into the mud, her screams overriding a new chant that shattered the night: *Bite. Bite. Bite.*

Kathryn's feet tangled in the roots of a tree and she slipped and fell to the ground, ramming her knee against a cypress tree. The mud splattered her clothes and face, but at least she'd lost the snake.

Two arms wrapped around her and pulled her to her feet. "How'd you get here?"

"Roark. I should have—"

"Not now, Kathryn. We've got to get out of here. Fast. Before the crowd realizes I'm helping you, instead of capturing you. Do you have a car?"

She nodded. "A rental. Green Ford Escort. On the road. In the back."

He took her hand and started running in that direction, pulling her along. She heard Veretha screech in the background. When she glanced back, two men were chasing them, gaining ground. Roark picked up the pace, not slowing until they reached the car. She tore the keys from her pocket and tossed them to him.

She jumped into the passenger seat just as the first man lunged for her. Luckily he slid in the mud and missed her. Roark revved the engine, put the car in drive and sped off, leaving a stream of flying mud, which hit the man who'd lunged at her squarely in the face.

Once they'd put a couple of miles between them and the meeting site, he reached over and laid a hand on her shoulder. "Do you have some kind of death wish?"

Kathryn started to tell him she didn't have to explain her actions to him, that she'd been through enough. She couldn't. She was shaking too hard to form the words.

"Aren't you supposed to be the practical sister who doesn't take risks?"

She nodded and found her voice. "Most of the time I am."

"Why couldn't I have known you then?" He pulled her close with his right arm. She didn't even think about pulling away.

Trust. Lies. Deceptions. They'd seemed a barrier impossible to cross a few hours ago when she argued with Roark about Raycine. Now all that mattered was that Roark was here. She didn't understand him, didn't understand herself anymore, but she knew she felt safe in his arms. Right now that was all that mattered.

"YOU CAN TAKE a hot shower first," Roark said as he unlocked the door to his apartment and opened it for Kathryn. "I'll make some hot chocolate to warm you up."

"I'm not cold."

"You're shaking."

She looked down. "So I am."

He walked with her to the bathroom, making sure she was steady. "The towels and washcloths are in the same place they were this morning. Help yourself. Do you need anything out of the car?"

"My handbag. I have a toothbrush and toothpaste in there."

"I'll get it for you."

She nodded. As soon as he left, she stripped out of

her wet, muddy slacks and sweater and stepped into the shower. The hot pulsating spray kneaded her back and shoulders. She stood there and let her muscles unknot before she set about the task of scrubbing the mud from her hair and face. By the time Roark returned with her handbag, she'd finished her shower and wrapped herself in a towel.

"This is where I came in before," he said.

"I'll tie the towel tighter this time."

"I doubt that would have helped this morning."

She doubted it would help tonight, either, except that she was so sore, she wasn't sure she could function. Strange, no matter how strong the doubts and uncertainties that reared up between them, there was always an underlying attraction and bond that seemed to draw them back together.

She couldn't imagine standing in a small bathroom, dressed only in a towel with any other man. Yet, here she was, and it felt perfectly natural. But then, after visiting in the worlds of Devlin and Veretha Tishe, anything not totally twisted and bizarre might seem natural.

"Your hot chocolate is in a mug on the table by the bed. Anything else I can get you?" he asked, already stripping out of his mud-splattered shirt.

"A massage would be good."

"Coming right up. Just let me wash off a layer of scum first."

She finished brushing her teeth and padded down the hall to the bedroom, leaving Roark to his shower. Unanswered questions still rambled through her mind, but not with the urgency that had fueled them before. It was too late to catch a plane back to Dallas tonight, but there were regular flights out in the morning. She'd be at the attorney's office when Lisa came in to pick up her check.

But Kathryn had made a decision on the way back from Algiers tonight. If Lisa needed her and wanted her help, she'd be there. If not, she was going to back off. She couldn't live Lisa's life for her forever, couldn't be her conscience or her constant rescuer. It wasn't fair to either of them.

Her mind drifted back to Roark. Her feelings for him were strong, yet she still knew so little about him. Something had changed his life nine months ago, something that still hurt so badly he found it difficult to talk about. Had he lost someone he loved to Devlin Tishe? Or maybe *loved* was the wrong tense. Perhaps he was still in love.

VERETHA WAS SEETHING as she drove back into town. How dare Roark desert her and run to rescue Kathryn Richards! But it didn't matter now. She'd show him. And she'd show Devlin. While they slept, their precious Lisa Morland would be going on a journey. After that, if they wanted to see her, Devlin would have to summon her spirit from the world of the dead. As if he could.

Devlin the master. Devlin the devil himself, except that the only powers he possessed were all too mortal and all too fallible. What a shock it would be for him to discover that without her or Lisa's money, he was merely a man.

KATHRYN WAS in Roark's bed, lying on her stomach, her eyes closed, the towel still wrapped around her like a sarong.

"Masseur at your service. Just like you ordered."

"I could get used to that kind of service." She opened her eyes and noticed a bottle of some colored liquid in his hand. "What's that?"

"A love potion, compliments of Mystic Isle." He turned it so that he could read the small print on the label. "Heat and massage into the body of the person you are trying to enchant. Vary your stokes and leave no part of the body untouched. The magic in the oil will dissolve all resistance."

He dropped to the bed beside her, poured a slow stream of oil into his hands and rubbed them together. "Just relax, the magic in the oil will do the rest. It comes with a guarantee, and no one's ever come back for a refund."

"I'll bet not."

He placed his hands on her shoulders and then began to dig his finger into the flesh and aching muscles. The heat seeped into her body and awakened a longing so intense she trembled. If they continued like this, they'd wind up in each other's arms making love. It would be wonderful, but wouldn't answer the question that haunted her thoughts.

She rolled over.

"That wasn't much of a massage," he said, meeting her gaze.

"Do you care about me, Roark?"

"I'd think that would be pretty obvious by now. I got the impression you shared the feeling."

"I do, but I don't really know you."

"And you still don't trust me?"

"The problem is that you don't trust me, Roark. You give just so much and then you hold back the rest."

"What is it you think I hold back?"

"What happened nine months ago that made you

give up your life and move to New Orleans? What is it that torments and drives you?''

Roark exhaled sharply. He wasn't good at talking about feelings. He'd never shared the depth of his heartbreak at losing Margie with another living soul. Had never wanted to until now and wasn't sure he could do it. But he did want to, and that was a major step.

Kathryn reached over and slipped her hands into his.

He held them tightly. Waiting wasn't going to make this any easier, so there was nothing to do but plunge in. ''I had a daughter. She was sweet, smart, sensitive, the kind of daughter every father wants. Her mother died when Margie was only four, so it had been just the two of us.''

''You must have been very close.''

''She was my life. That's why it was so difficult for me when she graduated from high school and wanted to go away to college. But she'd been offered an academic scholarship to Tulane University in New Orleans, and her heart was set on accepting it. She was eager to move from our home in the mountains of northern Georgia to the Big Easy. I never felt good about the move, but everyone said I was being far too protective.''

''What did you do in Georgia?''

''I taught economics at a small college. I was on the executive fast track before my wife died, but I gave that life up so that I could have time to raise my daughter. I never regretted that decision.''

''But Margie accepted the scholarship and made the move.''

''Couldn't wait. She was very independent. The first semester all she talked about was school. The second semester she became enthralled with a doctrine of peace and harmony.''

''Obviously she'd met Devlin Tishe.''

He nodded. ''It sounded a lot safer than the other things I'd worried she'd get into in the big city, so I didn't complain. I figured it was some new-age philosophy that appealed to college kids, a stage she'd go through and outgrow. Unfortunately she never had the chance. I got a phone call from the Plaquemines Parish Sheriff's Office in March. My daughter's body had been pulled from the Mississippi River south of New Orleans. She'd been murdered, but no arrests were ever made.''

Kathryn felt his pain searing through her, as piercing as if it were her own. Now she understood the bond that had seemed to exist between them from the very beginning. It was pain and fear and mistrust of Devlin Tishe. All those things and more.

''I should have seen it coming. I should have stopped it.''

She blinked back the tears that burned at the back of her eyes. ''It wasn't your fault, Roark. You couldn't have known.''

''I'm not so sure of that. If I'd paid more attention to what she said, if I'd come down here and checked on her... But I did nothing. And I lost her.''

Kathryn put her arms around him, the last fragments of doubt seeping from her. She held him close for long minutes, stroked his back, bathed his neck in her own salty tears.

Then she poured a dab of oil into her palm and began to rub it into the tight muscles of his back and shoulders. Slowly the tenseness melted, and he lay back on the bed, pulling her down beside him.

They made love, different from the way it had been that morning—gentler, slower, but no less fulfilling. The passion dipped deep inside her, penetrating to every lonely chasm of her soul and satisfying needs she hadn't known existed.

"I love you, Kathryn."

She wanted to say it back. It seemed right to say it back, but she hesitated. "How do you know it's love, Roark?"

"Because I've loved before."

"And your feelings for me are the same as they were for Margie's mother?"

"No, Kathryn." He kissed the tip of her nose and then her mouth. "Loving you is different from anything I've ever felt before. You're different. I'm different now. But I know love when I feel it, and I feel it with you."

She snuggled into his arms, thrilled again to feel his hard body against hers. "I'm not sure about love, Roark. All I know is that I've never felt this way before, and that I want it to last forever."

"Forever works for me."

LISA AWOKE to the sound of a car pulling into the drive of Tujacque's Manor. She rushed to the window, thinking it must surely be Devlin. He'd probably told Veretha he was leaving and was coming to spend the rest of the night with her.

But it wasn't Devlin who stepped out of the car. It was Veretha, dressed in white veils that caught the wind and flapped like hungry seagulls. She never came to the plantation at this time of night, and there was only one reason she'd be here now. She must have found out about her and Devlin, and she was coming to stop Lisa from going away with him.

Lisa grabbed her cell phone and punched in Roark's number as Cottonmouth's heavy footsteps sounded on the stairs. The phone rang.

Answer. Please answer.

The footsteps were in the hall now, coming closer, almost to her door.

"Roark Lansing."

"I'm in trouble, Roark. Veretha's here. I think she's going to kill me."

The door burst open and Cottonmouth stamped inside. "You made a mistake, Lisa. Veretha doesn't tolerate mistakes."

ROARK DROPPED the phone, jumped out of bed and started throwing on his clothes.

Kathryn swung her feet to the floor. "That was Lisa on the phone, wasn't it."

"Yeah. Veretha just showed up at the plantation house where Lisa is staying. I'm going to check on her."

"I'm going with you." She yanked on her panties and slid her legs into the muddy green slacks.

"I'd rather you stay here."

"But you know I won't."

"I figured as much."

Kathryn was carrying her black pumps as they ran out the door and jumped into Roark's car. Her heart was pounding, her insides tossing like a rowboat caught in a hurricane. She was finally going to see Lisa. Only, odds were it would be too late.

Roark filled her in on the few missing details about Raycine's death as he raced down the highway, then took the dark curving back roads to Tujacque's Manor. Roark had sensed Raycine was becoming increasingly disenchanted with Devlin. He'd approached her with his concerns, and she'd agreed to hack into the computer files and see if she could uncover any incriminating evidence.

The night she'd disappeared, she'd tried to call, but the connection had broken up and he couldn't understand a word she said. He'd driven to the plantation that night, but Cottonmouth said that Raycine had left in a blue car with some friends of hers. He claimed he'd tried to stop her, but she'd sneaked out of the house, anyway.

That was the same night Kathryn had gotten the call warning her that Lisa was in danger. The scream that Kathryn had heard had probably been Raycine's last. The girl had been a friend right to the end. She'd make sure Detective Ranklin knew that.

The plantation house was dark when they arrived and the driveway was empty. If Veretha had been there, she'd come and gone. If Lisa was there, she hadn't called back.

"I'll do the talking," Roark said as he jumped out of the car.

Good. At this point Kathryn would never be able to get words past the clog in her throat.

ROARK WAS JUST ABOUT to find a way to break in when Cottonmouth finally lumbered to the door and opened it a crack.

Roark planted his foot in the crack. "Where's Lisa?"

Cottonmouth stroked his whiskered chin. "Up in her

room I guess. Where else would she be this time of night?"

"I want to see her."

"Since when did you start giving orders, Roark?"

"Since now." He pulled a pistol and shoved the barrel into Cottonmouth's belly.

"You gone crazy?" But the big man moved out of the way.

Roark grabbed Kathryn's hand with his free one and pulled her along behind him as he bounded up the stairs and headed for Lisa's room. It was empty. The sheets were thrown back, and the room showed no sign of a struggle. Of course, there would have been plenty of time for Cottonwood to straighten it between the time of Lisa's call and now.

The giant of a man was standing in the doorway to Lisa's room, breathing heavily from his fast climb up the steps. Roark pointed his gun at the man's head. "Start talking, Cottonmouth. Where did Veretha take her?"

"I don't know what you're talking about."

Roark rested his finger on the trigger. "I think you do. You have one minute to start talking before I shoot."

Cottonmouth's face twisted into hideous angles, his eyes wide and wild as if he was losing control. He lunged at Roark. She heard the gun go off, saw the smoke, smelled the sickening odor of gunpowder and fresh blood.

Her heart plunged and she grabbed the post of the bed for support. But it was Cottonmouth who staggered backward and fell to the floor.

Roark ran to him, checked his pulse and then turned

pale. "It just went off," he said. "I didn't mean to kill him."

"If you hadn't killed him, he would have taken the gun and killed you. I'm glad he's dead." Then it hit her. Now there was no one to tell them where Veretha had taken Lisa.

VERETHA DROVE SOUTH down Highway 23, headed toward the tiny town of Venice. From there she'd get Dan Brady to motor them out to Skull Island. It would be cold and deserted in December, the perfect place for a murder, Veretha-style. Not quick. Not easy. Death should be lingering for people who deserved to die.

Lisa moaned in the back seat of the car. Veretha had thought she'd shot her with enough drugs to keep her unconscious until they reached Venice, but apparently she hadn't. Still, Lisa's hands and feet were tied. She wasn't going anywhere.

"I'm sorry, Kathryn," Lisa mumbled. "I didn't want the dog to die."

Evidently she was still under the influence, Veretha thought.

"Don't tell Mom and Dad. They'll be mad at me. I hate for them to be mad at me."

Stupid muttering. If Lisa kept this up all the way to Venice, it would drive her nuts. She might have to stop and give her another injection to shut her up.

"I'll go back to Dallas with you, Kathryn. Come and get me. I'll go back."

Kathryn. Dallas. The older sister who lived in Dallas was named Kathryn. Kathryn Richards. Kathryn Morland. One and the same? Veretha beat her fist against the steering wheel, knocking the car off course and practically off the shoulder of the road.

Kathryn Richards had waltzed into Mystic Isle and into Devlin's arms much too quickly. That should have set off a few alarms. Veretha couldn't be sure they were one and the same, but it was definitely a possibility and would be easy enough to verify. And if Lisa and Kathryn were sisters, she'd do them a big favor. She'd let them die together.

Too bad she couldn't have her followers around to watch. It would be one of her crowning moments.

Chapter Sixteen

Kathryn stood at the window in Roark's kitchen, staring at nothing. She'd made coffee, wiped off the counter, thrown a load of towels in the washing machine, even taken out the trash. Busy work, but if she stayed idle too long, her rattled nerves would drive her totally nuts.

Lisa was out there somewhere with a crazed voodoo priestess, and no one had any idea where to look for them. Not even an authentic voodoo priestess, according to Roark. Veretha had put her own twist on the ancient rituals and convinced a ragtag group of followers that she had powers to cast or repel spells. She was basically a snake handler with a dramatic flair and the ability to lead a group to the edge of frenzy.

She'd walked a thin line for the past few years, balanced sanity with madness, order with chaos, lucidity with delirium. Now she'd crossed the line, and Roark admitted that he had no idea what she was capable of at this point. The only man who might be able to reason with her couldn't be found. Devlin Tishe had apparently packed his most expensive clothes and moved out of Mystic Isle.

Roark had driven down the bayou, hoping to find

Yvonne and see if she had any idea where Veretha might have taken Lisa. This time Kathryn was forced to stay behind. They'd called Detective Ranklin when Cottonmouth was killed and filled him in on everything that had transpired tonight.

He was picking up a search warrant now. When he got it, he wanted Kathryn to go with him to Mystic Isle and help him search the records for anything that might sound familiar to her. He was looking for the name of any place Lisa had mentioned. That would at least give them somewhere to start looking.

But deep down she had a feeling they were all just humoring her, when they really believed Veretha had already killed Lisa and disposed of the body. But as long as there was a ghost of a chance that Lisa was alive, Kathryn wouldn't give up hoping or doing everything she could to find her.

She poured another cup of coffee and took it to the living room. Her phone rang. She prayed it was good news as she punched the talk button. "Kathryn."

"Kathryn Morland, how nice to hear your voice."

"Who is this?"

"Don't you recognize me? No, I guess you wouldn't. It's my husband you've spent all the time with."

"Veretha."

"My, but you're perceptive. You probably already know what I want."

"Whatever you want I can get it for you. I just want you to release Lisa."

"I don't think so, Kathryn. Lisa and I are having a little party at sunup. We'd love for you to join us, and you will if you want to see Lisa alive again."

"Let me talk to Lisa."

"She's not too coherent right now, but if you listen very carefully, you can hear her hallucinating."

"Mommy, make Kathryn...play. I don't...alone."

The words were slurred so badly that Kathryn could barely make them out. But it did sound like Lisa, talking in the helpless voice she'd used when they were young and Kathryn hadn't wanted to give in to her.

"Where are you, Veretha?"

"We're going on a little boat trip. You can come, but you must promise to come alone. If you bring anyone with you, even Roark Lansing, there will be only two of us left to enjoy the party. And you probably wouldn't have nearly as much fun if that happened."

"How do I find you?"

"Follow Highway 23 south. You can reach it from the Westbank Expressway. Just stay on the highway until you reach the town of Venice. When you get there, go to Guilbeaux Bait, Tackle and Marina. A man named Dan will be waiting to bring you the rest of the way."

"I'm leaving now, Veretha. I'll be there as soon as I can."

"Tell no one, Kathryn. This is a score for the two of us to settle. And come alone, or you will be partying with Lisa's corpse."

The connection clicked off. Kathryn scribbled down the directions Veretha had given her. She had no illusions about what Veretha had in mind. Whether she went alone or not, she would kill both of them. She punched in Roark's number.

"We are sorry, but the customer you are calling is not available. Please try again later."

Panic time, but she couldn't afford to lose her cool. Roark was probably in one of those isolated areas

where there was no provider to carry the call. But if
he was, he'd be back in a coverage area soon. She
grabbed the keys to her rental car and a windbreaker
Roark had left on the back of one of his kitchen chairs.

She'd try him again in a few minutes, but she
couldn't just hang around and wait for him to drive all
the way back into town. He'd have to meet her in Venice. It would be the fastest way. Besides, he'd know
how to handle Veretha's request that she come alone.

A few minutes later, she was on the interstate heading back toward the Mississippi River. She took the
map of Louisiana from the glove compartment and
tried to read it as she drove. Highway 23 ran along the
river. She'd reach Venice just before the Mississippi
emptied into the Gulf of Mexico at the lower tip of
Plaquemines Parish.

Venice, Louisiana. Guilbeaux Bait, Tackle and Marina and a man named Dan. And a killer of a party
with Veretha Tishe. It made Mystic Isle and its appa-
ritions from beyond the dead seem tame.

YVONNE AND ROARK paddled the small pirogue down
a shallow bayou so thick with vegetation that at times
it was hard to propel the boat through it. They slowed
again, then came to a stop. Roark picked up the long
pole and planting it on the bayou bottom, pushed as
hard as he could. The boat finally inched forward. "Are
you sure we can't get to this man's house by car?"

"It is hard, I know, but Simon never want to live by
the road. He cut himself off from us long ago. But he
knows things about Veretha. He knows them from long
ago, from before she marry the man with silver hair
and lying tongue."

And Simon might be the only man who could help

Roark. Yvonne had told him about an island somewhere in the Gulf of Mexico that Veretha visited in the
dead of winter for some sort of ritual of passage.
Yvonne had no idea how to find the island, and neither
did anyone who worked for her or lived around her.
Simon was his last hope.

"Simon will not be happy I brought you to his
place."

"I appreciate your doing it."

"I owe you, Roark. After this, the debt it be paid in
full, no?"

"There was never any debt, Yvonne. I did what I
had to do."

"You stepped in and saved my Michelle from the
crazy man. I always pay my debts, Roark. Yvonne be-
holden to no man. You know me. It's not my way."

"We'll be even," he said, knowing that was the reassurance she wanted. And he had saved Michelle from
a crazy man the very first night he'd gone with Veretha
to a séance deep in the bayou country. Some guy had
gotten high on booze and decided Michelle was the
woman who had left him for another man. He'd tried
to throw her into a roaring fire. Roark had stopped him
just in time.

"We got very close now, Roark. That shack, down
yonder in the trees. Simon live there. He's a strange
man, that one, but he know stuff about Veretha. I tell
him you're my friend. He help you."

Roark hoped that was true. He took out his phone
and tried to call Kathryn just to let her know he was
still working on tracking down Veretha. He punched
the talk button, but the dial stayed dark. Surely he
hadn't switched off the power. He tried to turn the

phone on. No response. What a hell of a time for the phone to curl up and die on him.

"Your phone, it work fine, Roark. Just not here. Mine, neither. This whole area is what they call a dead zone. No one can use the cell phone. The Cajun folks who live back in here say it's an omen."

An omen in the pitch-blackness of night on a lonely bayou. Roark didn't want to think what kind of an omen it might be. He just wanted some answers and to get out of here fast. He didn't like being cut off from Kathryn, not even for a minute. And it was likely he'd been cut off for a lot longer than that.

He'd asked Kathryn to call when Ranklin arrived. That should have been at least an hour ago. His phone hadn't rung once.

But Simon's shack was only a few yards away. It was too late to turn back now.

VERETHA TUGGED a semiconscious Lisa from John Brady's fishing boat. She'd known he would lend it to her. She and John went way back. He was one of the original members of the Skull Island Solstice group. He and Dan. Friends you could count on in a crunch.

The police could come around all they wanted when she was through. Neither of them would ever let on that she'd been here. It would be the perfect murders. The Morland sisters would just disappear. It would serve them right and give Devlin exactly what he deserved. Nothing.

She half dragged Lisa across the mud. There was little grass. No trees. No light except the beam from her flashlight. And in the middle of the small island was a small shack, just big enough for what she had planned. The torture of two people who deserved to die.

She had the ropes, the drugs, the needles and the snakes. She'd even brought the torches. It would be a ceremony to remember for the rest of her life. Veretha Adoradan Tishe. From a street kid in a New Orleans ghetto to the reigning queen of the damned.

The only bad thing was that none of her friends would be here to see the performance. Not even Devlin. And he was the one who had started it all. Started it when he brought in Raycine and when he started spending too much time with Lisa.

IT WAS TEN MINUTES before three in the morning when Kathryn drove up to Guilbeaux Bait, Tackle and Marina. There were no lights in the shop and none on any of the fishing boats moored behind the weathered building. She killed her lights and lowered her window. The wind blowing across the river was cold, and though she couldn't see the Gulf of Mexico, she could smell the saltwater.

Roark hadn't called back, but she'd left a message, telling him exactly where she was going.

"Miss Morland."

She jumped, slamming her elbow against the steering wheel.

"I didn't mean to startle you."

She turned and saw a tall skinny man dressed in a gray slicker, jeans and white marsh boots. "Are you Dan?"

"Yes. Veretha said you'd be needing a ride to Skull Island."

"Is it far?"

"An hour in a fishing boat like mine. We can start whenever you're ready."

She climbed out of the car. The cold penetrated the thin windbreaker. "Which boat is yours?"

"The shrimper over there." He nodded to an old boat docked at the end of the wharf. "It ain't fancy, but it'll get you there."

Get her to Skull Island. All she had to do was climb on board. But it would be a one-way trip with no hope of return. Roark could find her here at the marina, but how would he ever find her at Skull Island?

"If a person doesn't have a guide, how would he find Skull Island?"

"Don't know that anyone would want to."

"But if he did want to. Could most people around here tell him where it is?"

"One or two could, but they wouldn't."

"Why not?"

"Skull Island ain't a real name. It's the name the Solstice group gave it. Don't no one call it that but us. And we don't tell."

But he was telling her, apparently sure the secret would be safe. She'd be going to Skull Island, but she wouldn't be returning. Neither would Lisa. "Is there something special going on at Skull Island tonight?"

"It's a party. I hear you're one of the guests of honor."

Yeah, well, she wasn't going, not unless someone knew where she was. If she climbed in the boat with this guy, she'd just be joining Lisa in certain death.

"I need to make a call before I go." She reached inside the car and pulled out her cell phone. Dan yanked it from her hand and flung it as far as he could. She watched the surface of the water break as it hit, the ever-widening circle of the ripples marking the spot.

She yanked open the car door, but Dan kicked it shut, barely missing her fingers. A second later she felt the sting of his hand across her face. She tried to fight back, rammed a fist into his gut and clawed at his face with her fingernails. Blood dripped from the cuts and ran down his chin and onto his jacket, but still he threw an arm around her chest.

She tried to break away and run. The butt of his flashlight caught her on the side of the head. Her knees buckled and she felt herself falling. Before she reached the ground, he'd hammered the flashlight against the back of her head. A river of sticky blood ran down her neck and under her collar, and she sank to the ground in a heap.

When she came to, she was sitting on the cold planks of the deck, her hands and feet tied with a thin cord that cut into her flesh. The smell of dead fish was nauseating.

"Guess we're going to the party," she said.

"Just about there. If you look to the left, you'll see the glow of the torches. Looks like the hostess is all ready for you."

DAN SHOVED Kathryn across the island, sometimes with the palm of his bony hand, sometimes with the heel of his boot. He'd untied her feet but left her arms tied behind her. If she'd had any strength left, she might have been able to make a run for it, but her head was spinning crazily, and she could barely make her feet keep moving. Besides, she was on a tiny island in the Gulf of Mexico. Where would she run?

Finally Dan stopped shoving and let her fall to the

ground. The torches were a few yards in front of them, surrounding a dilapidated shack that looked ready to cave in at any second.

"I got your guest out here, Veretha. What'll I do with her?"

Veretha stepped out the door. She was still dressed in the white veils, but they were smeared with mud and blood. Kathryn's stomach jumped, twisted, turned inside out. It had to be Lisa's blood. "What have you done with my sister?"

"She's waiting for you, Kathryn. You're all she's talked about. She's so anxious for you to join her at the celebration. But Lisa has a new name. She's Lizemera now. The chosen one. Devlin's favorite, at least she was until you came along."

Dan backed away. "Well, they're all yours, Veretha."

"Don't you want to stay for the celebration?"

"No. I got a wife now and a kid on the way. I can't afford this kind of trouble. But you go for it. You were always different from the rest of us. Even when we were kids growing up in the projects, you were different. Weren't scared of nobody 'cept your dad. That man had a whooping hand on him. When he got after you, I could hear you yelling from three buildings away. You coming back for the Winter Solstice?"

"No. I won't be coming back at all."

Dan shrugged and walked away. Kathryn liked the odds a lot better now. She tried to stand, but the world rocked and she fell back to the ground. Veretha grabbed her by the shoulders and dragged her past the torches into the circle of light and then into the shack. There were no windows, though there were enough boards missing to let in the light. She scanned the area until she caught sight of Lisa, sitting in a chair in the corner.

Her eyes were closed, but Kathryn saw the steady rise and fall of her chest and knew she was alive. Tears pooled in her eyes, then ran down her cheeks, mixing with the fresh mud and the dried blood. She must look a sight. Not that it mattered. No one would ever see her.

And she would never see Roark again. She wished she'd done a better job of telling him goodbye. Wished she'd told him she loved him.

Lisa opened her eyes and stared at Kathryn. "Is that you?"

"It's me, Lisa."

"I'm sorry, Kathryn." Her voice was strained and weak. "I'm so sorry. I never meant to drag you into this."

Kathryn tried to focus, but her head kept falling forward. The best she could do was stare at the floor.

"You didn't drag me into this, Lisa. You told me to stay away."

"But I knew you'd come. You always come. Why do you?"

"I don't know, Lisa. I really don't know. I guess in spite of all we've been through over the years, I love you. You're my sister."

"Sisters to the end." Lisa sniffed and closed her eyes. "Do you think Mom and Dad can see us now?"

"I think so."

"They're probably sorry they had me. I was never as smart or as good as you were. Now I'm the reason you're going to die before you've really had a chance to live."

"That smarter and better bit. Did you think that when you were growing up?"

"Always. Didn't you?"

"Never once. Not in all my life." Sisters, but they'd never really known each other. Too bad. They might have been great friends.

Lisa closed her eyes. "It's not long until sunup. That's when Veretha is going to kill us. It's the time when the world is in the best alignment for death. Did you know that?"

"No, and I still don't." But sunup was near. The blackness beyond the torches was turning gray. Any minute now the first glow of the sun would creep past the horizon. Then Veretha would carry out her quest born of madness, and Lisa and she would die.

On Lisa's twenty-fifth birthday.

Veretha should be preparing for the ceremony now, but she was slumped in a chair, her head down, snoring softly. Kathryn stretched and realized her head had finally stopped spinning. She stared out a hole where a board had rotted away. Some of the torches had gone out, their supply of fuel exhausted.

A shadow crossed the opening. It had looked almost like a man. She held her breath, afraid to hope. It moved again, and this time Kathryn caught a glimpse of Roark's face. Her heart jumped to her throat and almost stopped beating.

There was no way for him to find her, and yet he had. Veretha was stirring, waking up, her fingers still wrapped around the handle of the black pistol. If she woke up and saw Roark, she'd shoot him in a New York minute. Kathryn had to do something to get her attention, to give Roark the advantage.

She rocked forward in her chair. The back legs came

off the floor, then resettled with a thunk. Veretha jumped up, spun around and stared straight at Roark.

"Welcome to the party, Roark. But you don't have to die with the Morlands. I can shoot you right now." She pointed the gun at his head.

Kathryn threw herself forward, falling face first on the floor. The gun went off, a crashing sound that seemed to explode inside her head. Blood was everywhere now, running in streams across the cracks in the floor. Her stomach hurt. She was going to be sick. And she was going to pass out.

"Hang in there, Kathryn. I'm coming for you."

The voice floated above her like one of the voices in the Awakening Room.

"Oh, no. Don't die, Kathryn. Please, don't die. Not now. Not after all of this."

Lisa was calling to her, but Kathryn ignored her. She tried to see Roark through the blur that covered her eyes, wanted to get up and help him, but her side hurt too much. She put her hand to the pain and into the bloody cavity where the flesh had been blown from her body.

Noise exploded inside her head. Voices of the spirits, all talking to her at once. Detective Ranklin. Lisa. Roark. She had no idea what they were saying, but someone was holding her close.

"I love you, Roark."

"Then don't leave me, Kathryn. Please don't leave me."

She held tightly to his hand so he could help her stay. It was all up to him. She was too weak to fight on her own. The voices grew louder, became a horrible roar. And then she drifted away.

Chapter Seventeen

Lisa rode back to town in the helicopter with Ranklin and Veretha. The pilot had first airlifted Kathryn to a hospital in New Orleans. Roark had flown with her.

Veretha patted down the white veils and finger-combed her hair. "You can't take me to jail," she jeered, staring at Ranklin. "I haven't done anything."

"Sure I can. Margie Slaton's dead. My daughter's dead. Now I catch you red-handed trying to kill Lisa and Kathryn Morland."

"But I didn't kill Margie, and I didn't kill Raycine."

"Yeah, that's what they all say."

"But I didn't. Devlin killed them. If I had killed them, do you think you'd have found their bodies so quickly? He didn't even get Raycine to the river, just panicked when she almost escaped and dumped her in the first water he came to. He would have probably fouled up Lisa's murder, too, if he'd had to kill her to get his greedy hands on her money."

Lisa reeled at the words. They were all lies. Devlin wasn't a killer. They were going to Paris. Tomorrow. No, today. It was her birthday and she was about to become a very rich woman. She wouldn't need allowances or stipends anymore. She could live her life any way she pleased, and she pleased to live it with Devlin.

"So if you didn't kill Margie and Raycine, you better have some pretty convincing proof of Devlin's guilt."

"I have all the proof you need. It's at Tujacque's Manor."

The veins in Ranklin's neck stood out. "Why did he kill Raycine?"

"The same reason he killed Margie. He had to. They started to doubt him and went snooping. Little vixens. They came on to him just like Lisa did. Came on to him and then turned against him. I didn't kill them, but they deserved to die."

"Is that why you were going to kill Lisa and Kathryn?"

"I would have killed them because they deserved to die, not because they knew too much. Lisa is the most gullible of all. She actually thought Devlin was going to go away with her. But it was only her money he was taking."

"No. That's not true. Devlin loves me. We have tickets to Paris. We're leaving today."

Ranklin shook his head. "Devlin isn't going anywhere except to jail. But I can tell you that he never had tickets to Paris. He had one ticket for himself under the name of David Tishe. He was flying to the Cayman Islands and from there to Rio."

She wanted to scream at Detective Ranklin, to shout that he was wrong. Only, shouting wouldn't change anything. All the other accusations rang in her mind. Had Devlin killed Raycine? Did she just want so badly to believe him that she ignored all the signs?

"Tell me Devlin didn't kill Raycine, Veretha. Please tell me he didn't."

Veretha sneered.

Lisa turned to Ranklin. "You don't think he did, do

you, Detective Ranklin? It is Veretha who is evil. Devlin is good.''

"I'm sorry, Lisa. If you ask me a question, I have to answer you honestly. I believe that Devlin Tishe is guilty of murder in the first degree. But don't be so hard on yourself. You were only one of many to be taken in by him.''

Devlin, a killer who'd used her and planned to steal her inheritance. She didn't want to believe it. It made her look like such a fool.

She didn't want to believe it, but she did. And it hurt so badly she could have cried. Only, she didn't. If she was going to cry at all, it would be for Kathryn. She closed her eyes and saw the blood in her mind and the gaping tear in her sister's stomach. Then she bowed her head in the noisy airplane and prayed that her sister would be all right.

Kathryn was all the family she had left, and she loved her.

ROARK AND LISA sat together in the hospital waiting room, neither of them talking, though he was glad she was there. He wasn't sure he could have gone through this alone. He'd thought last night had been the worst kind of nightmare, but he'd been wrong. This morning was far worse.

Last night at least he'd been doing something. Today there was nothing he could do but wait and pray. Kathryn's life was in the surgeon's hands. And in God's.

Lisa leaned forward in her chair. "How did you find us last night, Roark? Veretha was certain no one would tell you where to search. The people who knew were all sworn to secrecy.''

"She was almost right. I spent more than half the night chasing a phantom, a man who was supposed to know all. Turned out, all he knew about was Veretha's past. Fortunately for us, Ranklin found one person who'd actually been to the ceremony at the island before and was brave enough to talk.''

"Was it anyone I know?''

"She told Ranklin she met you once when you were down in the French Quarter with Raycine. A spunky little homeless kid with bright-red hair. Goes by the name of Punch.''

"I do remember her. Called Punch because she can deliver one when she has to. At least that's what Raycine said.''

"Anyway, to answer your question,'' Roark went on, "I got in touch with Ranklin when I finally got Kathryn's message. I was already in Venice when he called me back with the information about how to locate Skull Island. I borrowed a speedboat.''

"I heard you stole it.''

"Stole. Borrowed without asking. It's just semantics. Anyway, I took the boat. Ranklin came by helicopter. You know the rest.''

He stood and paced the room. Only, they didn't know the rest, wouldn't until they got some word on the success of the operation and whether or not any of Kathryn's vital organs had been injured beyond repair. He'd known her only a few days, but now he couldn't imagine life without her.

For nine months he'd focused on nothing but getting Devlin Tishe. The man had been arrested at the airport an hour ago trying to leave the country, but the victory was hollow for Roark. All that mattered now was Kathryn's pulling through the operation.

"How did Ranklin know to contact Punch?''

"A hunch. A good detective's stock-in-trade,'' Ranklin said, striding into the waiting room. A skinny girl with bright-red hair was with him. "I brought her along today for good luck. Besides, she's got a stake in this. She wants to be here to pull for the patient."

Lisa got up and gave her a hug. "Thanks, Punch. I guess you never know where the next miracle is coming from."

Roark still paced. "I thought we'd know something by now."

Ranklin patted him on the shoulder. "Take it easy, buddy. Falling apart won't help anything."

The door swung open. The doctor stepped inside. Lisa rushed to him. Roark backed away. He'd waited all morning for this, and now that the time was here, he was so scared he couldn't even make his gaze meet the doctor's.

"It looks good. The next twenty-four hours are critical, but it looks good."

Lisa squealed and ran to hug Roark. He just stood there stiffly.

"She's asking for Lisa and Roark," the doctor said. "The two of you can go in, but only for a few minutes. She's going to need lots of rest and a great deal of care."

ROARK MANAGED to pull himself together somewhat before he faced Kathryn. He took her hand and held it in his. "Hi, there."

"Hi, Roark."

Lisa moved in closer. "You did it again, sis. But it's the last time you'll have to come in and rescue me, and that's a promise. I'm doing a complete turn-around."

"Good."

"I may even come back to Dallas and work if you can find a place for me in the company."

"I'm sure I can. You can take over some of my duties. I think I'm going to be very busy for the next few years."

"I think so," Roark agreed. "I have lots of plans for you."

Lisa stepped back. "Wait a minute. You two are acting very strange. Is there something going on here I should know about?"

"Could be," Roark said. "There just could be."

"I think maybe I should leave the two of you alone." Lisa backed out of the room.

"The doctor said I can only stay a minute," Roark said. "He doesn't want me to tire you out."

"Roark Lansing, man of mystery." Kathryn spoke so softly he had to bend low to hear her. "Did I ever tell you that I love you?"

"Once," he answered, "but you can do it again— anytime. I guess it was that love potion we used for your massage."

"Do you believe in magic?"

"I do now, Kathryn. I definitely believe in it now. And I am completely under your spell."

"So what do you think we should do about that?"

"Marriage comes to mind."

She closed her eyes, then opened them slowly. "If that's a proposal, I accept."

"Marriage and happily ever after and a couple of kids thrown in for good measure." She didn't hear the rest of his words. The pain medicine had taken effect and she had drifted back to sleep. It didn't matter. He had the rest of his life to love her. A man couldn't ask for more than that.

HARLEQUIN®
INTRIGUE®

**brings you a new miniseries from
award-winning author**

AIMÉE THURLO

**Modern-day Navajo warriors, powerful,
gorgeous and deadly when necessary—these
secret agents are identified only by the…**

In the Four Corners area of New Mexico, the elite investigators
of the Gray Wolf Pack took cases the local police couldn't—
or wouldn't—accept. Two Navajo loners, known by the code
names Lightning and Silentman, were among the best of the
best. Now their skills will be tested as never before when
they face the toughest assignments of their careers. Read
their stories this fall in a special two-book companion series.

WHEN LIGHTNING STRIKES
September 2002
NAVAJO JUSTICE
October 2002

Available at your favorite retail outlet.

HARLEQUIN®
Makes any time special ®

If you enjoyed what you just read,
then we've got an offer you can't resist!

Take 2 bestselling
love stories FREE!

Plus get a FREE surprise gift!

Clip this page and mail it to Harlequin Reader Service®

IN U.S.A.
3010 Walden Ave.
P.O. Box 1867
Buffalo, N.Y. 14240-1867

IN CANADA
P.O. Box 609
Fort Erie, Ontario
L2A 5X3

YES! Please send me 2 free Harlequin Intrigue® novels and my free surprise gift. After receiving them, if I don't wish to receive anymore, I can return the shipping statement marked cancel. If I don't cancel, I will receive 4 brand-new novels each month, before they're available in stores! In the U.S.A., bill me at the bargain price of $3.99 plus 25¢ shipping and handling per book and applicable sales tax, if any*. In Canada, bill me at the bargain price of $4.74 plus 25¢ shipping and handling per book and applicable taxes**. That's the complete price and a savings of at least 10% off the cover prices—what a great deal! I understand that accepting the 2 free books and gift places me under no obligation ever to buy any books. I can always return a shipment and cancel at any time. Even if I never buy another book from Harlequin, the 2 free books and gift are mine to keep forever.

181 HDN DNUA
381 HDN DNUC

Name	(PLEASE PRINT)	
Address	Apt.#	
City	State/Prov.	Zip/Postal Code

* Terms and prices subject to change without notice. Sales tax applicable in N.Y.
** Canadian residents will be charged applicable provincial taxes and GST.
All orders subject to approval. Offer limited to one per household and not valid to current Harlequin Intrigue® subscribers.
® are registered trademarks of Harlequin Enterprises Limited.

INT02

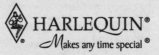

DISCOVER
WHAT LIES BENEATH

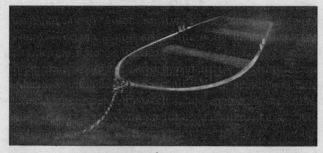

by
USA Today Bestselling Author

ANNE STUART
JOANNA WAYNE
CAROLINE BURNES

Three favorite suspense authors will keep you on the edge
of your seat with three thrilling stories of love and deception.

Available in September 2002.

HARLEQUIN®
Makes any time special®

Visit us at www.eHarlequin.com

PHWLB